HURRY UP
HARRY HANSON

HURRY UP
HARRY HANSON

MEL ELLIS

FOUR WINDS PRESS   NEW YORK

By the same author

Run, Rainey, Run
Ironhead
Sad Song of the Coyote
Softly Roars the Lion
Ghost Dog of Killicut
Wild Goose, Brother Goose
Flight of the White Wolf
The Wild Runners
When Lightning Strikes
Caribou Crossing

Published by Four Winds Press
A Division of Scholastic Magazines, Inc., New York, N.Y.
Copyright © 1972 by Mel Ellis
All rights reserved.
Printed in the United States of America
Library of Congress Catalogue Card Number: 76-182121

For the men and women of the Wisconsin Department of Natural Resources

HURRY UP
HARRY HANSON

ONE

Men call the muskellunge many things, among them Spade Face. And though it is an uncomplimentary designation, it fits, because his face is, of course, long and flat and slightly concave—just like a garden spade.

But there the resemblance ends, because in the dished-in face there is a pair of glaring, and what some might call, evil eyes.

Except that it is hard to think of a fish as being evil. Mostly, all muskellunge prefer to live in peace. But stories get started, and Fish Fins (Jim) Larrens, a guide, swears he saw a muskie cut through a group of bathers, lacerating three with its long teeth.

"I'm telling you, it was like watching a shark," Fish Fins would tell the story, though, of course, he had never been near salt water, or ever seen a shark. Well, maybe

9

it was true. Fish Fins knew his muskies, of course. But he liked to tell stories too.

Of course, there are days, or even seasons, when maybe the moon, or something else, is just right, and then old Spade Face will chase beavers, muskrats or just about any swimming thing, even though he already is glutted with chubs, shiners, suckers, or whatever else is available.

Biologists are aware of the unpredictability of Spade Face, and it is one of the headaches they have in trying to propagate muskies artificially. Since a muskie will eat nothing which isn't alive and moving, biologists claim that a wash tub of hungry young ones, all of the same size, will keep eating one another until there is only one left.

Naturally this has nothing to do with the muskie in this story, because Spade Face of Bloody Burn Bay never saw a wash tub, but was born in the mud.

Bloody Burn Bay? It's a part of Turnabout Lake, a body of water which winds almost back on itself. Some say the bay got its unusual name during a forest fire back before the time many people lived in northern Wisconsin. A fire, sweeping through the trees across the bay, cast such a brilliant reflection on the water that a fire fighter, recently emigrated from England, shouted: "The bloody bay is burning!"

Anyway, everybody called it Bloody Burn Bay, and the important thing is that on a certain spring day in nineteen hundred and twenty-seven Spade Face wriggled from a yellow egg in the mud, swam upward a few inches, and then sank back to the bottom to take energy from a little sac which was attached to his belly.

Prophetically, on the same day Spade Face was hatched, the wife of a young fire tower watcher who lived on the shores of Bloody Burn Bay, suddenly realized the baby she was carrying wouldn't wait and meant to be born whether she was ready or not.

So Hurry Up came squawling into this world without anyone in attendance, and his mother might have died giving birth, if Goose Gait Goetz, a neighbor, hadn't come by with a gift of just-picked mushrooms and found the pair.

Goose Gait wouldn't even have gone into the cottage when no one answered the door, except that he heard the baby crying and the woman moaning. So he burst through, and when he saw the two of them on the bed, he said:

"Oh Lord, Ethereal, what's happened here?"

"Get a doctor, please, Mr. Goetz. Get a doctor," Ethereal had moaned.

Goose Gait, who is a forester and fire fighter, always claimed afterward: "I guess I cut down about sixteen poplars and maybe twenty young maples getting around the corners with that truck. And I made Doc ride back with me, and he never looked up once, but kept his head in his hands all the way back."

Of course, Hurry Up wasn't the baby's real name, but the people of the Bloody Burn Bay area had a sense of humor, and, maybe to try and make light of what might have been a terrible tragedy, they nicknamed the boy Hurry Up.

But then, everybody in the Bloody Burn Bay area had a nickname. It showed they belonged. It meant they were loved, and where city folk might call someone "Darling" or "Luv" or "Sweetheart," these people of Bloody Burn Bay had special names like Fish Fins or Goose Gait or Bear Paw or High Pockets or Step-an'-a-half . . . or whatever fit, or sometimes didn't fit.

All except Ethereal Hanson, Hurry Up's mother, and everyone called her Ethereal or Mrs. Hanson. She never used nicknames. With her it was always Mister Goetz or Mrs. Larrens—never Mister Goose Gait or Mrs. Fish Fins.

It was her proper Boston upbringing, and it seemed she could never quite do what people called "settling in." Perhaps it was because she was already a grown woman when she left Boston, and the Back Bay breeding was in her blood.

Actually Hurry Up's real name was Harry, after his father, and though this story has mostly to do with Hurry Up and Spade Face, the muskie, it was a long, long time before they met.

Life for Hurry Up, during his early years, was never so perilous as it was for Spade Face, although Hurry Up did have a habit of leaping without looking. There were trees he shouldn't have fallen out of, a skunk he shouldn't have petted, a gun which kicked him off the porch when he tried to shoot it, a dunking in the lake before he'd learned to swim, a hornet house he shouldn't have poked with a stick, and such other relatively minor crises as beset a boy who is in a hurry to live all his life in the first three or five or ten years.

But if life for Hurry Up was a series of mishaps, life for Spade Face was a minute-by-minute, hour-by-hour, day-by-day duel with death. Perhaps this accounts to some degree for the fact that Spade Face was endowed with a savage sense of survival. And, in a way, maybe it was just such a sense of survival which saved Hurry Up Harry Hanson from dying during his premature birth or later breaking his neck or drowning.

While still an egg, and then before his egg sac was absorbed, Spade Face couldn't help himself. But once the egg sac was gone he wriggled out of the mud and darted into the nearest jungle of weeds where it would take a pretty agile fish to catch and eat him.

Already, even then, he had it over Hurry Up, because Spade Face could take care of himself whereas Hurry Up couldn't even walk, much less swim, and if his mother hadn't nursed him, he'd have died.

What's more, Hurry Up was something of a lumpy caricature of what he'd look like later when he was grown, because he was round, fat, pink, and often moist.

But Spade Face was already an exact replica of what he would look like when he weighed five or ten or thirty pounds. Already his face had the dished-in look. The teeth, although he'd lose some and get others from time to time, were already arranged in lethal rows. Fins, tail, scales, eyes—all were perfect as they'd ever be. And if he was a shade lighter, with hardly any bronze glints to his green, slick body, that would come with age.

So while Hurry Up was luxuriating in a soft, warm crib and having his diapers changed, Spade Face was either being stalked by larger fish or was, in turn, stalking creatures smaller than he.

Of course, neither Hurry Up nor Spade Face had any idea they were what some people call star crossed. Loosely this means, if you believe in astrology, that the stars which were supposed to guide the destinies of both would bring them together someday.

Anyway, whether you hold with astrology or not, it is interesting to note that Hurry Up and Spade Face were, as you might say, hatched on the same day under somewhat perilous circumstances and right within shouting distance of each other. If you like, you might presume that the forces which guide destinies had something planned which included the two of them.

So perhaps it is not amiss, that in considering how Spade Face and Hurry Up came to be sworn enemies— at least Hurry Up came to hate Spade Face—we think a little about their earlier years, the years before they met.

There was, of course, a christening party for Hurry Up, and fire tower watchers, woodsmen, fire fighters and game wardens came to sample the cider.

High Pockets and his wife, Pee Wee, were there. The Loud Mouth Kids all came (they were called that because they were always so quiet, sitting like mice in a corner). There was the widow, Sugar Plum, who was anything but sweet. And also Bear Paw Svendson and Little Leak, the fire district clerk, Ham Hocks Garrity, Weasel McGlint, Four Toes Gregory (he'd cut off one in a logging accident), and lots of others, because back in 1927 before television and when radio was just starting to become popular, people still had time for each other.

So Hurry Up got a send off, even if he didn't know it, and it so happens it was on the same day that Spade Face absorbed the last of his egg sac and became a free-swimming fish.

But if Hurry Up had no worries except sometimes a gas bubble or the hiccoughs, Spade Face seemed to be forever on the run from something. The very first week he was a free-swimming fish, a banded perch chased him, and if there hadn't been a rock crevice to duck into, that would have ended it for Spade Face, and he and Hurry Up would never have had their terrible trouble.

Then the second week Spade Face was pursuing a cloud of daphnia (microscopic water creatures) which had schooled in a yellow cloud around what looked like a big, black rock. The tiny muskie had charged in, chomping down on daphnia, when suddenly the big, black rock moved and opened its jaws. Spade Face saved himself only because he gave an extra hard thrust with his tail, and swam out of the suction which the snapping turtle had created by opening its jaws.

But Spade Face's enemies weren't only fish and turtles. The big bullfrogs which lived in the rushes relished little fish, and there were also kingfishers on hovering wings, and terns swooping down from measured flight, and raccoons poking around through the muddy bottom with their five-fingered feet.

There were mink and otter, and even a muskrat wasn't above grabbing a little fish if it swam close enough. So Spade Face lived right on the edge of eternity.

All the while he was growing fast and Hurry Up wasn't even out of diapers when Spade Face was an eight-inch green jet who had given up eating daphnia and preyed on any fish smaller than himself, and sometimes ones which weren't.

He didn't even have to learn how to do it. It came, like the gift of sight. It was just there, and he'd lie in the jungle of grass looking like a slender, green leaf and if a fish swam by—zap, he'd have it, and he'd hold it crossways in his jaws and swim back into the weed jungle.

He'd hold the fish until he was pretty sure it was dead, and then he'd slowly turn it until the head was pointed toward his gullet, and then slowly he'd swallow it, and then position himself to pounce on another.

16

Mostly he was sensible enough to chomp only on victims smaller than himself, but one day he made the mistake of getting hold of a cousin who was a full inch longer. If he'd have dropped the larger fish and backed off to look for something smaller, it would have been all right. But there was something in his nature, which in humans might be called a stubborn streak, so he held on.

His teeth did their job all right, and he killed the muskie, but when he tried to swallow it, it wouldn't go all the way down, and there he was, swimming around with half a muskie sticking out from between his jaws.

And wouldn't you know it, but on that same day Hurry Up broke a piece of metal off one of his toys and it got stuck in his throat and he almost died!

Now that almost seems like more than coincidence. First being born on the same day, then the christening and free swimming coming together . . . and then this.

Well, anyway, Mrs. Harry Hanson had the sense to turn Hurry Up upside down and whack him a good one on the bottom, after which the piece came shooting out like a bullet.

For Spade Face it wasn't that easy, not having anybody to whack him on the bottom, so he went into the darkest corner of the weed bed, let himself sink until he could feel the mud touching his belly, and then he lay there gasping for water so that his gills might be able to put enough oxygen into his blood stream to help him stay alive.

For survival he could thank his gastric juices, which are about strong enough to melt iron. The head of the muskie began to digest, so Spade Face could swallow a little more. Then, slowly, a little more and a little more of the fish's body dissolved, until finally Spade Face, with a determined spasm, got the fish past his gills, and the oxygen-filled water rushed in to save his life.

So it happened Spade Face and Hurry Up survived to be ready for future confrontations. For Spade Face it was a coon, fishing in the shallows, but he slipped out of its paws and dived for water deep enough so that even the moon beams couldn't find him. And for Hurry Up it was falling out of his high chair and landing on his head.

Then Hurry Up got the measles and was all speckled, and Spade Face became the host of a number of tiny water fleas, and they looked like measles marks.

So it went, and at the end of the first year Spade Face was ten inches long, and Hurry Up was crawling all over the kitchen floor. At the end of the second year, Spade Face was fifteen inches long, and Hurry Up was walking.

In the ensuing years Hurry Up fell out of a tree and a boat, petted the skunk, and all the rest of it, while Spade Face nearly got lifted into the sky by a fish hawk, and only escaped an otter because he put up a mud cloud while high-tailing it across a shallow bar.

Then by the fifth year Spade Face was big enough to quit worrying about other fishes, and most predators (except man, of course), because he was twenty-seven inches long and weighed a little more than five pounds.

Hurry Up, though of course not yet a man, wasn't hanging to his mother's apron strings any longer. At four feet, he weighed sixty pounds, could swim almost like a fish, and row a boat from Bloody Burn Bay all the way around Turnabout Lake to where the tamarack swamp was a dark and mysterious place even in full sunlight.

TWO

For years then, both fish and boy lived uncomplicated but exciting lives, getting larger and smarter. So it was they came to their tenth summer —the critical summer when their stars crossed.

That tenth summer, as it turned out, was about the driest that northern Wisconsin, or maybe any part of the middle west, had ever experienced. The lake dropped, and the rivers ran almost dry. The sky was a bronze shield, and the sun a blazing white disc. The grasses turned brown, and where dirt showed through it was cracked like a fire fighter's hands.

There were fires in some parts of the north almost all the time. The air was acrid. Smoke put a haze over the forest. The muskie eggs which were laid that spring never hatched, because the mud they were laid on lifted into the sun before they were ready to pop, and the birds picked them up.

20

Though it was a deadly serious thing, the people of Bloody Burn Bay did not lose their sense of humor. Goose Gait Goetz claimed that a crew of bullfrogs stole some of his shovels to dig a channel from Turnabout Lake to a pothole back in the swamp to get some water to their pollywog kids who lived there. And Bear Paw Svendson claimed an osprey broke its neck diving after a fish because the creek had turned to steam and only looked like water.

Ham Hocks said the raccoons were getting drunk because berries were fermenting and turning to wine right on the vine, and High Pockets claimed that a bear which lived nearby made a water canteen out of a gourd so he could carry it and have a drink when he wanted one.

But for all the stories about the birds eating their own eggs because they fried before they could hatch, and about the wild vines that crawled a couple of miles to get water, these men of the north did not take the drought lightly, but fought with every resource at their disposal to save the forests from being leveled by fire.

Hurry Up hardly ever got to see his dad, Harry Senior (called Step-an'-a-half when his wife, Ethereal, wasn't around), because he was off watching for or fighting fires, unless he needed a change of clothes or something more to eat.

Only once did all the men take off work. They met on the shores of Bloody Burn Bay at Hurry Up's home (because it was the most centrally located), in order to make plans for evacuating the women and children if the fires came close.

There were the three conservation wardens: Shoot First (Sam) Canuck, who had never fired a gun; Siren (Joe) Click, who always blew his siren when he passed his girl's house; and Two Gun (Dave) Fry, who had never owned a firearm.

There were others who Hurry Up knew better, like his godfather, Goose Gait (George) Goetz, the man who waddled when he walked and had saved Hurry Up's life the day he was born. And there was the widow Sugar Plum (Sarah) Sack; High Pockets (Ray) Forsythe and his wife, Pee Wee; Bear Paw (Sorensen) Svendson; Little Leak (Larry) Lane; Ham Hocks (Gerald) Garrity; Weasel (Mack) McGlint; Four Toes (Pat) Gregory; Fish Fins (Jim) Larrens; and some others Hurry Up didn't know so well because they lived on the outskirts of the Bloody Burn Bay country.

They made Bear Paw's wife chief of the evacuation crew because she was the biggest and could holler the loudest, and because she wanted to be. Then the other wives were assigned certain jobs if flight became necessary. Some were designated as Paul Reveres to ride the countryside giving the warning in case the fire cut the telephone lines, and only Shoot First's wife didn't get a job, because she was pregnant, and they didn't want to burden her further. Hurry Up's mother, Ethereal, got the job of looking out for Shoot First's wife, in case they had to make a run for it.

It was all a great lark for the boy. And though he knew he'd get thrashed for even thinking it, Hurry Up did kind of play with the idea of the fire coming, because he thought it might be great fun to go racing off in pickup trucks out ahead of the flames with everybody shouting and sweating and swearing.

But mostly the threat of fire hadn't concerned him, because it was that time in his life when he was too enthralled with the things which were going on in the water and the woods and the meadows to concern himself about such a remote threat as a forest fire.

He had stood that April on the shores of Bloody Burn Bay to watch the muskies churn the water in their orgy of spawning, never knowing, of course, that Spade Face had come with the other males to fertilize the golden eggs.

Already Spade Face was a sleek arrow of a fish, weighing nearly fifteen pounds. He was bright green with glints of bronze on his scales, and he made quite a showing as he came nosing up to the flats of Bloody Burn Bay when the water temperature reached fifty degrees.

Then, when he found a big female muskie almost three times as heavy as he was, he began following her and nudging her with his long, concave snout.

Apparently she didn't mind the nudging, because she

stayed around, and then Spade Face, in what appeared to be a thrust of exasperation, rammed her good and hard in the side and she rolled over, and a golden trickle of eggs began pouring from a vent near her tail.

At once Spade Face lay over on his side, and a white fluid began squirting from a vent near his tail. In this way he was adding to the sterile eggs sperm which would fertilize them so they'd grow into baby muskies.

From the shore Hurry Up saw the muskies writhing, and he knew what was going on, because his father had told him about fish spawning, and the year before he had watched the little bluegills come to their white pebble nests, and saw the little flatties—all gaudy in their marriage colors—go through the wedding dance which insures survival of the species.

Sometimes the big muskies became so excited the water boiled, and the female spread a quarter-of-a-million eggs over several acres before she had spent herself. Then Spade Face turned away to go to deeper water, and Hurry Up left the pier to go exploring in the woods.

Gradually, then, spring turned into summer, and by then Hurry Up had a sister, a pink baby with soft, yellow curls.

In the heat, Spade Face had discovered the shade of the Hanson pier, and he had decided that this would be his lair. Beneath the pier the water was a few degrees cooler, and it was always dim down there out of the reach of the sun. What's more, perch, chubs, shiners,

24

suckers, young muskies, walleyes—lots of little fishes—had a natural inclination to come to the pier for precisely the reasons Spade Face liked it, so he didn't have to go far for food.

Then one day Hurry Up was standing on the pier wondering what to do next, when he saw a swirl and then a boil of water right below, and he knew, of course, that it had been made by some big fish. So he lay on his stomach and hung his head over the side to look beneath the pier.

Of course, it was too dark to see much, especially after having been squinting into bright sunlight. But he knew that his eyes would adjust soon enough and he'd see, if not clearly, at least somewhat better.

Even so, it took him a long time to spot Spade Face, because the muskie had let himself sink close to the bottom in the darkest shadows. But finally his eyes could pick him out, and though he could not clearly define such things as pectoral fins, or see the glaring eyes, he could see the muskie's outline and he knew that he was a substantial fish—nothing really big, but getting there.

Hurry Up watched awhile, but the muskie never moved, so at last he got up. There were red marks on his ribs where the pier slats had pressed into his chest, and one arm ached from having been folded for so long.

But Hurry Up never noticed such things, because already at ten years of age he had grown into a buckskin bootlace of a boy.

So he went to the house, and, though he would have preferred to tell his father about the muskie (because he so rarely saw him during these critical days), he confided in his mother. "A muskie has taken to living under the pier," he said.

"Oh?" Ethereal answered. She answered mostly with questions these days, because she was worried about the fires which seemed to be everywhere, and because she rarely got to see her husband. So she answered with a lift of her voice, a questioning lilt, and this saved her from any long talks and allowed her to think about things she considered more important.

So Hurry Up talked instead. "Yes," he said, "looks to be about a fifteen pounder. Down next to a piling in the shade. Suppose the water is so warm even the fish like to get into the shade."

"You think so?" Ethereal asked.

Hurry Up didn't feel like playing the game of answering questions, because his mother wasn't listening anyway. So he went outside again, and went around to the shady side of the white cottage and sprawled in the dust.

He was about to get up and go for a walk along Bittersweet Creek to see if there might be any fish up in the pockets back of the rocks, when his mother called:

"Harry!" Then (with that questioning lilt): "Harry Hanson?" He waited to see if it was important enough for her to call a third time. When she did call again with an edge of exasperation in her voice, he got up and walked to the door.

"Come on in," she said, "a mouse has built a nest in the back of this cupboard and she's got young in it. I want you to help me."

Now this was something Hurry Up knew something about—mice. He got to his knees and thrust himself half-way into the cupboard. There, behind some old pails and a pan or two, was the mouse nest of shredded paper, all round and neat and compact.

He spread it carefully, and found five mice all furred, with eyes open and bugging out, all of them ready to establish their own territories in any part of the cottage not already occupied.

"What do you want me to do with them, Mom?" Hurry Up asked.

"I want you to put them into an old pail and take them out and drown them," Ethereal Hanson said.

Hurry Up didn't much like drowning mice. He would rather have taken them into the woods and played with them for a while and then let them go.

Maybe his mother knew, because she said: "And I mean drown them, because if you don't they'll be right back in the house again, and if there's one thing we don't need, it's more mice."

"All right, Mom. All right," Hurry Up reassured her.

He closed the mouse nest carefully, slid both hands

beneath it, and in a single motion he had nest and mice in one of the old pails. Then he backed out of the cupboard, got to his feet, and started for the door.

"Now you drown them, Harry Hanson Junior," she said. She never called him Hurry Up like everybody else did. Usually it was Harry. If she wanted to make a point of something, she'd say Harry Hanson. And if she *really* meant it, she'd say Harry Hanson Junior—with emphasis on the Junior.

So Hurry Up knew she meant it, and that she might even watch from a window to see that he did the job. He carried the pail of mice down to the pier and debated whether he should toss out nest and all as far as he could, or take the mice from the nest and put them to the water one by one.

Drowning mice didn't seem cruel to Hurry Up, because the deaths of animals and birds were a normal and necessary part of living. In the fall his father shot ducks, deer and grouse. During the winter months when it wasn't necessary to be in the fire tower, and if he wasn't cutting pulp logs, he might run a trapline. So Hurry Up had seen muskrats, beaver, otter, fox, coyote—all manner of animals—killed in many different ways.

Hurry Up did, however, have an aversion for killing anything that wasn't going to be used. If the meat of the animal could be eaten or its pelt sold, that made sense. But song birds, for instance, why kill them? Dead, they weren't good for anything. Alive, they could sing. It was the same with the mice. What could you do with a dead mouse? At least a live one was something to watch.

But Ethereal had said to drown them, so he spread the nest at the bottom of the tin pail. He reached down taking one of the small mice by its tiny tail, held it up to the sun, and gave it a flip.

It didn't go out into the water as far as he had planned, and was swimming feebly back toward the pier. He got to his knees to watch, and the mouse, paddling frantically with its very small feet, made a tiny V through the bright placid water.

It was doing very well when suddenly a dark shadow lifted from beneath the pier. Even before Hurry Up's eyes could focus, there was a big boil of water with bubbles running in all directions, and the mouse was gone.

The muskie!

Hurry Up remembered all the stories about how hungry muskies might tackle a young beaver, and how even a small deer might get a leg torn if it swam over a lair. But he had never seen it happen to anything before, and now he sat back on the pier utterly amazed at the speed and dexterity of the fish in scooping the mouse from the surface.

When he had recovered, he reached down for another mouse and gave it a short fling. It too paddled frantically for the pier, and zap!—the muskie had it.

Well, that was something, and in Hurry Up's mind it was a fine bit of conservation. The mice weren't being

wasted but were serving a good purpose, that of furnish-
ing food for a fish, and above all, a muskie—king of the
fresh water fishes!

Spade Face took the other three mice in quick succes-
sion, and Hurry Up wondered where he could get some
more mice. He took the pail back to the house and
poked around in the cupboards, but, finding nothing, he
went back outside. In the forest he looked under fallen
trees, in brush piles, along the creek bank . . . but no
mice.

He wondered about frogs. Hurry Up knew a pothole
which still held some water, and an unusually large number of amphibians had congregated there because all
other marsh pockets in the area were dry. So he went
back to the pothole, which wasn't more than a quarter-
mile from the house. When he got down to the reedy
shoreline, frogs were poking their heads up through the
scum everywhere.

He knelt carefully, selected a victim, and then with a
quick grab had the slippery frog between his fingers. He
changed hands to get a better grip, and, holding the frog
by its long hind legs, trotted all the way back to the pier.

By the time he got there sweat was coming through
his blue denim overalls. He didn't wait, but tossed the
frog immediately out into the water. The frog, instead of
swimming toward the pier, swam away from it.

Spade Face came out anyway and with a jet-like burst
of speed closed in on the frog. Then, just at the moment

that he would have snapped his jaws over the swimming frog, it dove. Hurry Up saw the muskie recover instantly, turn abruptly, and start for the frog, which was diving for the protection of the mud at the bottom of the bay.

Hurry Up could see it all as plainly as if he were looking through a just-washed window. The frog, kicking frantically to reach the bottom so it could dive into the mud. The muskie, poised for an instant, and then moving swiftly downward on the frog. It was exciting—this race of death—the most exciting thing Hurry Up had ever seen. And all of a sudden he was rooting for the frog, hoping it would get into the mud in time to escape the jaws of the fish.

But it didn't. Just at the last second, the muskie had it. There was a swirl of mud as the fish's tail stirred up clouds of silt as it turned to keep from ramming into the bottom.

When the silt settled, the muskie was nowhere in sight. Hurry Up got to his stomach and leaned over to look beneath the pier. After a while he could see the muskie. It was in the same dark place, the shadowy place alongside the piling, lying so low it almost touched bottom.

He sat up and with the sweaty sleeve of his blue shirt tried to wipe the sweat from his forehead and cheeks.

What a fish! he thought.

Then he got up and went into the house to find a sock. He hiked back to the swamp, filled the sock with eight frogs, and went back to the pier to feed Spade Face.

Three of the eight frogs got away. Two dove so deep into the mud, Spade Face couldn't get them, and a third made it to a snarl of coontail moss, where the muskie would not follow.

That night Hurry Up had terrible dreams about a gigantic muskie which kept chasing him each time he went swimming, and Ethereal Hanson had to sit with him until he was awake enough to take an aspirin and a glass of water.

THREE

The drought continued. Now there wasn't even dew at dawn. Some days the sun was almost hidden by the smoke of fires which burned in so many places that some just had to be ignored. The fire fighters concentrated only on those which threatened villages or groups of cottages along the shores of the lakes.

Only the fact that each day dawned and died without a breath of air saved all of northern Wisconsin from becoming one fiery cauldron, roasting alive men and animals, and scorching the earth.

"If a wind comes up," Hurry Up had heard his mother tell the widow Sugar Plum, "we're all lost. There's nothing can save this country."

So they prayed for rain. And on Sundays, when Hurry Up went in the pickup truck to the white church at the crossroads, the only man there was High Heavens (Jonathan) Winterspoon, because all the others were out fighting fires.

So High Heavens (they called him High Heavens because one of his favorite expressions was "Mercy to high heavens!") prayed with the women, and he would intone:

"Oh Lord, please may this evil thing which has beset our beloved north country pass from us. Let this land with its thousands of jewel-like lakes once again live beyond fear.

"May You return our men safely to their hearths. May the fires which plague this, our earthly paradise, be wetted down and put back even as You kept the fires of hell from the doors of Your heaven."

After church there usually was a short meeting of the Women's Volunteer Evacuation Committee, and for ten or fifteen minutes Mrs. Bear Paw Svendson would talk about such things as the need to wet themselves thoroughly in case they had to make a run for it.

And she'd always say: "Be sure you've got plenty of blankets in the truck to wrap up in, and don't forget to tie handkerchiefs over your faces . . ."

One of those Sundays was the first time Hurry Up ever remembered his parents arguing. When they got home from church Harry Senior was there. He'd come for clean clothes and some rations. Hurry Up was on the porch, but he heard his mother say in a high pitched voice: "If you'd have only listened to me in the first place, we wouldn't be in such a dangerous predicament!"

But it was obvious that Harry Senior was in no mood for being badgered. He had been going days without sleep, and days with never enough food, and every day there had been unbearable heat and smoke and danger, and so he shouted at her: "If I'd listened to you, I'd be back in Boston wearing a stiff collar and sitting on a stool back of a bank window like some confounded monkey in a cage."

"Well, at least you'd be safe. We'd all be safe," Ethereal shot back at him.

"Well, if that's all life is about, being safe, then it doesn't count for much," Harry Senior said.

They talked so loud Hurry Up was embarrassed, and he left the porch and went to the pier hoping he couldn't hear. But his mother shouted so loud that he heard clear down to the pier.

"Oh, Harry, what have we got here! The children will grow up like little savages. They'll never see a museum or an art gallery or hear a concert. The only music they know about is that tinny jingle jangle that comes over the radio, and how can anyone call that music!"

There might have been more. But these days there wasn't even time for arguing, and Harry Senior had to jump into the state truck and get back to his post. But what Hurry Up had heard helped explain some of the things he had often wondered about.

Now he could better understand why his mother al-

ways called everybody Mister or Miss or Missus—
instead of Sugar Plum, Weasel or Ham Hocks—like everybody else did. Now he could understand a little what
his mother meant when she said, "back home."

He could also understand why perhaps she was sometimes so lonesome. He knew her parents, his grandparents, lived in the east, because she had always said that
someday when there was enough money they'd take a
train and visit them. And he remembered how her eyes
would turn misty when she talked about them and Boston, and how her work-weary shoulders would come
back, and she'd sit straight and prim and proper in her
chair while talking about the parties she used to attend.

So it probably was a hard life for her back in these Wisconsin woods, and Hurry Up could see how she might
not like being cut off from the rest of the world, no matter how beautiful her world in the woods was.

He was wondering what he might do to make things
easier for her when Goose Gait Goetz drove into the
yard, and, banging the pickup truck door, stepped out.

"Hya, Hurry Up!" he said, rather excitedly.

"Hya, Mr. Goose Gait," Hurry Up answered.

"I ain't got but a minute, but I got a present for you."
Then from beneath his shirt he pulled a tiny, fuzzy,
furred animal.

"A puppy!" Hurry Up exclaimed. Ever since he could
remember Hurry Up had wanted a pup.

"No, it's not a puppy," Goose Gait said. "It's a young

fox. Fire burned them out, but this one fell into the creek and lived." He handed the young fox to the boy.

The fox's puppy hair was just turning from a woolly fuzz into the slick, long, auburn coat which it would have as an adult.

"He can eat already," Goose Gait said, "so you don't have to bother with a bottle."

The young fox, which had snarled when first handed over to the boy, settled down in Hurry Up's arms. Apparently, after the terrible ordeal of the fire and falling into the creek, he was content to accept whatever attention was turned his way.

Goose Gait petted the fox's head. "You've got to watch him. He bites. But if you treat him gentle, feed him good, and love him a lot, he'll be your friend."

The boy was almost ecstatic. Suddenly he thought of Ethereal, and he swung his head toward the house just in time to see her bright, pretty face as she stepped through the door to see what Goose Gait wanted.

"Look, Mom . . . ," Hurry Up started toward her and then remembered that it was she who had said he couldn't have a pup. Suddenly he was afraid she might make Goose Gait take the fox back.

"How do you do, Mr. Goetz," Ethereal said. Blonde hair curled around her eyes, and Goose Gait seemed moved by her beauty.

"How do you do, Mrs. Ethereal," Goose Gait said, somewhat breathlessly.

37

"What's that you have?" Ethereal asked her son.

"A fox. Mr. Goose Gait gave him to me. A baby. A baby fox."

Mrs. Hanson stopped in her tracks. "You mean a *wild* fox?" She turned to Goose Gait.

"Well, he's not really so wild," Goose Gait said, "because he's only a baby, and he's lost his mother and father. They burned in a fire. And he's hungry, and he's scared, and he needs looking after."

"But, a *wild* fox!"

Hurry Up had visions of the fox going back underneath Goose Gait's shirt and being carried off. So he clutched the fox tighter, turned away from his mother, and, with his bare feet sending up little puffs of dust, ran around the cottage and off into the forest.

He went to Bittersweet Creek, and, where a huge hemlock leaned a hundred feet high, he crawled down among its roots into a small cave of sorts and sat in the shadows with the fox in his lap.

The creek, although a mere trickle in this time of dryness, was still energetic and made gurgling little sounds around rocks and among the roots which were as thick around as the boy's thigh.

There were birds sometimes briefly seen in the vault of leaves overhead. They were mostly silent these days, what with the heaviness of the air, and the mating season past, and the danger of fire hanging over their homes like the threat of doomsday.

He could see them: chickadees, whiskey jacks, robins, warblers . . . all almost solemn in their search for food, silently going along a dead branch to find a white grub. There was none of the twittering and chirping and occasional bursts of song which otherwise might have enlivened the July forest.

With one hand Hurry Up held the fox, and with the other hand he stroked it. Tense at first, the little animal finally relaxed in his lap. And Hurry Up remembered a piece of home-made maple sugar candy in his pocket. He got it out, peeled off the brown paper wrapping, and rubbed it gently across the fox's moist, black, button nose.

The little fox licked his nose, and the eyes came open with quick surprise. Hurry Up rubbed the fox's nose again, and once more the animal curled its narrow, pink tongue up to retrieve the trace of sweetness.

Then the boy held the small piece of brown candy so the fox could lick it, and the kit did, tentatively at first, and then with considerable appetite.

"But you can't have too much," Hurry Up said aloud to the fox. He had remembered Four Toes saying that sweets weren't good for dogs, so he surmised they probably weren't good for foxes either.

He stayed in the forest until shadows began to edge up from the low places, and then, with considerable misgiving, he started for home.

There was no one in the yard when he walked up. He

stood for a while wondering what to do, and then the door opened and his mother came out.

"Harry," she said, "didn't you hear me calling you?"

"No Ma'am, I didn't," Harry said.

"Well, I've been worried. Supposing a wind came up and the fires came in this direction. How would I find you?" She came close to him and stood for several seconds examining the fox kit.

"Can I keep him?" Hurry Up finally asked.

"For now I guess you've got no choice. We just can't turn him loose. He'd starve. If and when your father gets home, we'll talk about it."

Hurry Up beamed. The first hurdle had been jumped. He had temporary custody of the kit. Now, when his father returned, perhaps he'd have an ally. Then again, if his mother insisted that the fox go, his father might as quickly take her side just to keep peace in the family.

"You know supper has been waiting," Ethereal said.

"I'll be right in," Hurry Up said. He rushed around the house to the shed, dragged out a box, and put the kit into it. He was half-way back to the house when he went back, found some old boards, and put them over the box, though it wasn't likely the fox could have leaped high enough to get out.

That night he fed the fox left-over stew and some dry bread, and gave it a pan of water. He gathered dry grass and in the dark made a bed in one corner of the box. He had hardly finished when his mother called that it was time to go to bed.

He couldn't sleep. He saw the moon come through the perpetual haze of smoke which hung over the land, putting a subdued light on the tops of the trees. Once he thought he heard the fox whine, so he got up and, dropping down in front of the window, put his head on the sill and held his breath so he could hear better. He fell asleep there, head on his arms which were folded on the window sill, and when he awakened the moon had traveled over to the other side of the sky. He got up and walked stiffly to his bed and crawled in.

In the morning he was up as soon as day came streaking dirtily through the smoky sky. The fox was sitting up and whining when he pulled back the boards. So he went to the house, opened a can of condensed milk, poured half in a pan, and started toward the door with it.

He stopped when his mother's voice came from the bedroom. "Harry? Harry? What are you up to?"

"Feeding the fox."

"Feeding the fox what?"

"Condensed milk."

"Condensed milk? Well, all right."

Hurry Up breathed with relief and hurried out the door. When the fox wouldn't drink the milk, Hurry Up dipped his nose into it. The fox licked the milk off his nose. Hurry Up dunked the nose again. Again the fox licked it clean. Four times, and the young fox was lap-ping up milk as though he'd been doing it all his life.

When the milk was gone the fox looked at Hurry Up. He opened his long, narrow jaw, and, even though it was only to breathe, it seemed to the boy that the fox was smiling. In his delight Hurry Up almost laughed aloud, and a little squeak came from his lips. The tiny fox's ears came erect and he turned his head from side to side, much in the manner of a cat which is looking at a mouse it has been toying with.

Perhaps the fox had eaten mice. It would seem logical, Hurry Up thought, for the adult foxes to bring mice to the den site for the kits.

So Hurry Up went mouse hunting, and, when the arid earth yielded no mice, he chased a red squirrel into a hollow log. Then he put a bag over one end of the log and poked a stick in the other end. The squirrel jumped into the bag, and Harry squeezed it shut.

He doubted the advisability of giving a live squirrel to the little fox, but, having heard foxes were adroit killers, he dumped the squirrel from the bag into the box.

The little fox was overwhelmed. The chittering, chattering squirrel, scuttling like a little red rocket from one side of the box to the other, so frightened the fox that he went over backwards.

Hurry Up made a grab for the squirrel, but it ran up his arm, gave his ear a quick bite as it passed, and then, using his head for a launching platform, leaped to a tree.

Then it sat on a high limb, its tiny tail jerking convulsively, and gave the fox and the boy a tongue lashing.

The boy was no less astounded than the fox by the squirrel's acrobatics, and he sat back breathing heavily, fingering the ear which the squirrel had nipped.

It wasn't a bad bite, but there was a little blood, so Hurry Up decided against feeding the fox live squirrels, or any other live thing. He went to the house instead to beg a little fresh meat from Ethereal.

Ethereal said that fresh meat was a rare commodity because she couldn't get to the store every day, and often there was no ice. But she gave him some liver, and he cut it into tiny pieces, and then offered one to the fox.

The kit tasted it daintily, and then with a gulp swallowed it. The boy went off a little way, knelt and held out his hand, and called: "Foxy. Foxy." Then, when the fox came near, he fed him the meat. By noon the fox was following the boy wherever he went.

For the next few days the fox occupied all of his free time, and he couldn't remember when he'd been so happy.

Perhaps for the first time he realized that being a little boy back in the forest without playmates can be lonely. Up until now it had never occurred to him that he needed any one.

When school was in session there were, of course, other children. Even during the summers there was always enough to occupy him. When he wasn't doing chores around the house or yard, there were hundreds of birds to watch and scores of fish to catch. There was time for swimming, and time for climbing trees and touring the lake in his boat. So if anyone would have said that he was lonely, he wouldn't have known what they meant.

Now he would have understood. If, when his father came back, he was forced to part with the animal, he told himself he would run away first and take the fox with him.

His mother had been very kind, he thought. She gave him food for the fox and all the milk the little animal could drink. She didn't complain that the fox had a somewhat disagreeable odor—because most foxes do— nor did she say anything about getting rid of the animal.

But, of course, she never petted it, and though Hurry Up never noticed, she stayed at a discreet distance from the fox whenever the two of them were playing in the yard.

Harry Senior, gone for almost a week now, was due home any day. Ethereal took to looking up the winding road more often, and so did Hurry Up. He realized, of course, that when his father came home a decision would have to be made, and either the fox would be his friend forever, or he would disappear.

That night he was awakened by steps on the front porch, and then he heard his father's voice. His first thought was to leap from bed, to go running downstairs, to ask: "Dad, I've got a fox, and can I keep him? Please?"

But he restrained himself when he heard Ethereal's cry of delight: "Harry, you're home! Oh, Harry, it seems like a year!" Then he could hear that she was half-crying and half-laughing.

"I know. I know," he heard his father comfort his mother. "But it can't last forever. It has got to rain sometime."

And then it was quiet, and Hurry Up knew they were kissing. He allowed enough time for them to get the kissing out of their systems, and then he left his bed with a loud enough thump to warn them he was on the way down.

Half-way down the stairs, he saw them both standing together in the middle of the room. His father took a step forward and held out his arms. Hurry Up almost fell the rest of the way down, such was his eagerness to touch the big man.

At the foot of the stairs he slowed down, and by the time he got to his father he was in control of himself.

"Hya, Dad," he said, putting out a hand for his father to shake.

Instead, Harry Senior bent over and swept Harry Junior into his arms and hugged him.

It felt wonderful. It was much better than shaking hands. He was deeply grateful his father had made the move, because, of course, now he was old enough so hand shakes were in order. If there was any hugging it would naturally have to come from his mother.

When his father put him back down, he said: "Well, what's new, Son?"

It was his chance. "I got a fox, Dad. Mr. Goose Gait gave me a fox."

Harry Senior put a hand to his lips. "I thought I smelled fox when I drove into the yard," he said. Then he looked at Ethereal.

"It's a kit, a baby fox, Dad. A puppy fox."

"Where you keeping it?" the father asked.

"In a box in the shed."

"Bite you yet?"

"Once. Just a little. While it was eating."

"What do you plan to do with it?"

"Keep it," Hurry Up said, hopefully. "Make a pet of it."

Harry Senior looked at his wife, then back at the boy. "You know foxes can sometimes get pretty mean when they get older."

"But I can try to keep it tame. Can I try? Please?"

Again the father looked at the mother. "Well, we'll talk about it more in the morning," he said. "Now I've got to get some sleep. Seems like I haven't slept for a hundred years."

It was only then that Hurry Up saw the deep pockets of shadow beneath his father's eyes. It was only then that he saw the hollows in his cheeks, the whisker stubble on his chin, the blonde hair so dry it was sticking in all directions.

He saw then how the shirt his father was wearing was so stained by perspiration it might forever show the marks, and how the low leather boots, which some called bird shooters, were scarred and soiled by the fire.

Hurry Up started for the stairs. Then he turned. "I'm glad you're home," he said. "How long are you going to stay?"

"I have to leave right away in the morning. Things aren't good."

"Well, good night," Hurry Up said. He wanted to go back for one more hug, but he made himself go up the stairs instead.

"We'll talk about the fox in the morning," Harry Senior said.

FOUR

In the morning Hurry Up dressed quietly and crept downstairs and past his parents' bedroom to go outside. He didn't bother to take the fox his milk, but went to the edge of the forest to pick up several red pine cones. Then he went to get the kit out of the box.

He put the fox in his lap and began currying him with the cones. The little fox was almost ecstatic, such was his delight at being scratched. He stretched out full length while the boy ran the pine cones through his coat.

A louse scurried. Hurry Up quickly had it, and he cracked it between the nail of his thumb and forefinger.

It hadn't occurred to him that the fox might have lice. He parted the hair to examine the pup's skin. There were fleas too. He had seen them before on town dogs. It would never do to let Ethereal know.

Each time he found a flea, he plucked it free from the pink skin. They were ugly insects which looked like miniature crabs. First chance he got, he'd have to get some flea powder. He supposed he ought to worm the fox too. Goose Gait said that he used gun powder mixed with bear grease on his dogs. Maybe Goose Gait would help him delouse the fox and get rid of the worms—if the fox had worms—but then, didn't most young animals?

Perhaps he would walk over to Goose Gait's now, during this brief interlude before the sun became a searing white ball in the sky. He could be back before his parents got out of bed.

So he walked the Bloody Burn Bay trail with the fox following, and turned with every turn of the shoreline —along the path, under the spreading branches of hemlock and pine.

Mr. Goose Gait lived maybe a quarter-mile down the bay. Even if he wasn't home, Mrs. Goose Gait would know about the flea powder and the worm remedy, and perhaps he might borrow a little of each until he could go to the Twin Forks store to buy some and pay it back.

There were many animals and birds along the trail, because they had all gravitated to the shores of lakes and streams, what with their homes being burned out.

A buck in velvet antlers and a doe with two fawns ran from him, and then turned to look back. They were so close the boy could see the light shining in their dark, soft eyes.

There were beaver, and they rapped the water resoundingly with their tails and dove to go up the long, secret tunnels to their lodges on the shore. There was an endless procession of warblers so high in the trees that Hurry Up could only see their colors flashing. A pair of loons swam for deeper water, and a downy baby loon rode on one of the adults like a passenger on a speckled black boat. There was a mallard hen with seven half-grown youngsters just sprouting feathers, and a narrow, red-breasted merganser duck with a long, saw bill.

Then, even before he broke out of the trees into the clearing where Goose Gait's cabin stood, Hurry Up heard the hounds baying. They had scented him. He quickly bent over to pick up the fox.

There was no one in the yard and the truck was gone. That meant there was no one at home, because the rule was that no one should be left without transportation for even a short time lest the fire take a turn and come bearing down on them.

Hurry Up went closer anyway, just in case. The four hounds strained at their chains and sang out their old hunting songs because they smelled the fox.

The boy felt no resentment toward the dogs, because he knew that it was their nature to trail and catch, and their baying, though perhaps unseemly to an outlander, was one of the most ancient rituals attending the hunt.

When Hurry Up was a hundred feet from the front porch, and neither Mr. or Mrs. Goose Gait had come out to quiet the hounds, he knew they were not at home. So he turned and started down the path toward the bay. When he did so the hounds became frantic because the fox was moving away and they were helpless to follow.

They bayed louder, and threw themselves to the end of their chains. Hurry Up didn't have to turn to know that a swivel or snap had parted, because he heard the ping of metal, and he also heard the joyous uplift in one dog's bellow.

He turned, and there down the trail came a great golden dog with tremendous ears blowing back from the speed with which it ran. It was a jubilant hound, coursing along the scent line which lay on the heavy air. Here was a primeval creature carried forward by an instinct which went back a million years—the instinct to catch and kill.

Hurry Up clutched the little fox tighter to his chest and turned to run. But it was no contest, and the hound, unable to check himself, went dashing right between the pair. The hound had designs only on the fox, but its great weight sent the boy flying in one direction and the kit in another. The little fox recovered first, and, by the time Hurry Up was sitting so he could see, the kit was a flash of fur darting off into the brush. The hound had turned and was coursing down the hot trail of his quarry, giving tongue to the joy and savagery of it all so that the forest rang with his eloquence.

Back beside the cabin the other three dogs were hysterical because they'd been left behind. They squealed and yipped and hit the ends of their chains so hard that the breath was wrenched from their throats, pounded from their bodies.

By the time Hurry Up was on his feet and back on the trail, the baying of the hound was beginning to fade. Hurry Up raced in among the trees, and now he wished he'd worn shoes, because there were brambles in the clearings, sharp sticks where the young shoots of trees had died of thirst, and prickly pine cones.

But he ran regardless, always in the direction of the hound's baying, which by now had settled into a methodical, resonant roll—a sure sign the hound had settled down and that it would run forever, even through fire and flood.

Hurry Up ran until the lack of oxygen in his bloodstream pulled him up, and he leaned against the scaly bark of a red pine, gasping. It seemed the fox and hound were headed toward the fires, which he knew formed a rather indistinct line somewhere back along the hogsback of ridges which could be seen from any clearing.

He knew he should turn back and leave the fox to run as best he could to outwit or finally outrun the dog. But, he thought: Such a little fox! And such a big dog!

Why, the fox wouldn't know about back tracking, or taking to a creek, or running over the deadfalls, or along any logs—none of the tricks an older fox might employ to keep the hound from catching it.

52

And suppose, the boy thought, the little fox tries to return to its den. It would have to go right through the fire, because Goose Gait had said that the fire had killed the others, and this one had only been saved because it fell into the creek.

Hurry Up sobbed, but it was mostly because it was so difficult to get enough clean air into his lungs to ease the ache in his chest and the pain in his side.

Meanwhile the sounds of the chase receded, and, because he just couldn't stand there doing nothing, he started at a reasonable lope in the direction of the hound's baying.

That he was able to keep the sound of the dog's voice in his ears was due largely to the fact that there was no wind. Gradually his breathing returned to normal, and his progress was marked by a deliberate trot which never taxed him beyond his ability to keep moving steadily, always toward the sound, toward the baying of the hound.

Now there was an acrid tang to the air. He could taste fire on his tongue, and sometimes through a clearing in the trees he could see billows of smoke. The forest was becoming misty from smoke which came thinly through the trees.

Then at last he had to stop. The smoke was a biting presence in his nose and throat and lungs. It robbed him of oxygen, and he coughed, tried to spit, but his mouth was so dry there was no saliva.

If only he had a drink, but he could think of no creek

in this area. For that matter, he wasn't exactly sure in just what part of the forest he had arrived. The trees all had a sameness. They were huge, towering a hundred feet. Mostly all were red pine, only their crests still green.

He was debating with himself whether to continue on toward the line of fire when he thought the sound of the hound's baying seemed closer. He held his breath so it wouldn't interfere with his hearing. The baying did seem louder! Perhaps a breeze had risen, perhaps a wind was coming!

The thought of a wind struck terror to even his ten-year-old heart. He had heard enough about the savagery of a wind-driven forest fire, how it could go through the trees, leaping roads and rivers, even outrunning animals which had waited too long before fleeing.

But the dog's baying *was* coming closer. Maybe the little fox had come to the fire line and turned back. Perhaps there was no breeze after all.

He wet a finger with his tongue and held it aloft as his father had taught him. It did not become cool on one side more swiftly than on the other, so it was still calm. If there had been a breeze, the moisture on one side of the finger would have evaporated more swiftly than on the other. It would have made one side of his finger cooler. He would have known then that there was a breeze, and even from which direction it was blowing.

Now he could wait. The hound's baying was gradually

moving in a direction which he guessed would take the dog back to Bloody Burn Bay. After he was positive beyond a doubt that the hound, and presumably the fox, were headed back toward water, he began walking in the direction of the sound.

And now he began to wonder if he had been missed by Ethereal, or even if his father had wondered why he hadn't been around when he left to go back to the fire line. He hoped they hadn't noticed. But, of course, they would have missed him. If only they hadn't started to search for him, or alerted others in the Bloody Burn Bay area that he was missing.

It hadn't occurred to him before that he might be the object of a hunt, but he must have been gone at least two hours and, if they had missed him, he was sure they would become frantic when he didn't come running at their call.

The thought made him walk a little faster, and he hoped the hound was heading in the general direction of his home. It seemed that he was. The sun was to his right, and he guessed that meant he was heading back, because on the way into the forest the sun had been on his left. If he was heading back he should soon start to recognize land marks—see a tree he knew, a rock he could remember, or a swale he had once walked through.

By now he was so wet with sweat there wasn't a dry spot on him, and his throat was so parched it was only with difficulty that he could swallow. His nose, so dry inside it had cracked, was now bleeding a little, and he could taste the salty blood on his cracked lips.

His feet were bleeding too. Tough as they were from always running barefoot, there were tinges of blood on the tender toe ends. The legs of his overalls were torn where the brambles and branches had clutched at them.

But his misery was small compared to the misery he might be causing his parents, and his concern for their feelings was gradually taking precedence over his concern for the safety of the little fox.

Nevertheless, he followed the sound of the dog, because he didn't know in what other direction to walk. The character of the forest seemed gradually to be changing. It seemed he was dropping down, perhaps toward water, because the red pines were fewer, and there was more hemlock, and occasionally spruce and a birch or poplar grove.

Then, abruptly, there was Bittersweet Creek, and he ran to throw himself into the thin, silvery stream—to let the water cool his hot face, soothe his parched throat, curl comfortingly around the length of his body, from the dried ends of his hair to the tips of his bloody toes.

When he was thoroughly wetted, he sat up in the creek bed to listen. The hound was baying treed, and the sound was not too far distant.

He looked around to orient himself. He was on a far, distant part of the creek, one to which he came but rarely. He knew it was a good two miles from the bay, and from the clearing where his house stood.

Still he waited, because the hound was going nowhere. Either he had killed the small fox and was baying the corpse, or the kit had hidden in a hole or a crevice which was too small for the dog to follow.

Though reluctant to get up from the creek bed with its cooling waters, he pushed himself to his feet and sloshed along.

The sound of the hound's exasperated baying came closer and closer. Then, rounding a bend in the creek, the boy saw the dog. The little fox had taken refuge in the cave of roots beneath the hemlock which he had come to think of as his. Perhaps it was the odor (surely the cave must smell like him, he had lain in it so often) that had enticed the kit to seek refuge there.

"Hya! You! Slugger!" He thought the dog's name was Slugger. There was Slugger, Shot, Roundy and Pots, but sometimes he couldn't remember which was which.

"You! Slugger! Hya! Hya! Slugger!"

The dog turned his head toward the boy, and, anticipating help, he let out a wild yip.

"Git! Git! Git!" the boy shouted.

The dog looked perplexed. In bringing his quarry to bay he had done what was required, and he expected not only praise, but help in delivering the final blow. But instead, he was getting abuse.

The boy approached within ten feet of the dog. Beneath the hemlock roots, backed up into the black, cup-like depression, the fox was showing its tiny, white puppy teeth.

"You git, Slugger! You git!" The boy made a menacing gesture with his right arm.

The hound hung his head but refused to leave. Hurry Up considered for a moment. Then he bent down to pick up a stone the size of his fist. "See this, Slugger? See this? Now you git! Git! You hear me?"

The dog knew about stones in the hands of men and boys and knew they could hurt dogs. But he held his ground, tentatively baying at intervals, as though interceding with the boy to do what was now rightly his task—that of killing the fox.

"He's a pet, Slugger. He's a pet!" the boy implored. Then realizing the dog couldn't understand, he shouted: "Now you hound dog, you just git!" Hurry Up swung his arm as though to throw the stone. The hound cringed, but when the stone did not fly through the air, he seemed to regain some confidence and let go with a loud bawl.

"Okay, Slugger. Okay! You asked for it!" And Hurry Up threw the rock, but purposely threw it wide of the target, hoping to scare the hound off. It did not scare the dog, and, after giving the boy a look which was plainly questioning, he was back at the cave mouth bellowing.

The boy bent to pick another rock. The dog eyed him warily. "This time you get it, Slugger. This time you get it!"

Aiming carefully, but holding back so as not to harm the hound, the boy threw half-heartedly and the rock fell short of its mark. The dog jumped back a few feet, eyed the boy for a few seconds, and then dived back to where the fox was cowering. He began tearing at the hemlock roots with his teeth and throwing back sand and gravel with his paws.

"Slugger! Slugger! You no-good, egg-sucking hound!"

Hurry Up picked up another rock, and this time he did not hold back, but threw hard and caught the dog in the flank. The hound went over backward with surprise. Then, before he could recover, Hurry Up had another rock and pelted him for a second time.

It was too much for the dog, who had come to expect nothing but coöperation during the hunt. He started away through the forest, tail tucked under. Hurry Up followed up his advantage by throwing more stones and shouting: "Git! Git!" until the hound was out of sight.

Then he got to his knees in front of the cave, reached for the little fox, and got a bite for his pains. But he knew enough about animals to realize his pet was beyond comprehension and the bite was merely a protective reflex. So he reached in again, talking quietly all the while, and this time the little fox let him take him by the scruff and bring him out.

He sat with the fox in his lap pouring water over the animal's body. Gradually the swift beating of the little heart subsided. Then Hurry Up headed for home.

FIVE

Hurry Up walked carefully the last one hundred yards to where Bittersweet Creek skirted the clearing where the cottage stood. Carrying the fox now, he stopped often to listen, reasoning that if he had been missed and they were hunting him, he would hear the searchers shouting his name.

But there was nothing, and then, when he could see the house through a screening of alder branches, he wondered about all the trucks in the yard, and about the two automobiles, neither of which he had seen before.

He left the cover which hid the creek, and trying to appear nonchalant—as though he had only been out for a morning stroll—he approached the cottage.

A man in a business suit—necktie and all, in spite of the heat—was talking. Hurry Up stopped so he could hear better.

"It's for your own protection," the man was saying. "If a wind comes up, those fires might come right down on the bay, and then, well . . ." He spread his hands as though the Bloody Burn Bay people who were grouped about him understood only too well the consequences.

"Well, I don't know." It was Goose Gait Goetz talking. "I don't know if running now is going to solve it. If we leave the women and children here chances are pretty good they can hold off the fire at least until we get back to help them. Then we might be able to save the buildings."

Hurry Up saw his father step forward. "These," he gestured toward the house, "represent our savings. This is all most of us have in the world. We just can't abandon them. We have to at least try to save them. I agree with Mr. Goetz."

"And lose your lives in the bargain?" the man in the suit asked.

There were two other men in business suits, and they nodded in agreement. One of them said: "We're only trying to help. The situation is precarious. A wind and this bay area could become a holocaust."

Goose Gait was talking again: "I agree with Mr. Hanson. We just can't run. Not yet, anyway."

It was a strange sight on that searing summer day in the middle of the forest. Gathered there were all, or most, of the Bloody Burn Bay people in their old, work-worn clothes, some with the marks of fire fighting on their faces. And there—like people from some other world—stood the three men in business suits.

There was more talk, and the strangest thing was that all the Bloody Burn Bay people were calling each other Mister and Missus, instead of their nicknames.

Reflecting on it, Hurry Up remembered other times when strangers were present and how the people of the area did not use such names as Weasel, Fish Fins or Ham Hocks in their presence. Then it was always Mr. McGlint, Mr. Larrens or Mr. Garrity.

It pleased Hurry Up. In ways it was like a secret society, and there were probably few outside the Bloody Burn Bay area who knew they used such names as Shoot First and Step-an'-a-half. He thought it was good, though. It made them sort of select, members of their own special group. It emphasized their loyalty one to the other, and the nicknames were a continuing reassurance in the faithfulness of each to his neighbor.

"Well, we can't make you evacuate," the man, whose name Hurry Up now knew was Mr. Reese, said. "But as heads of the state departments in which most of you are employed, we felt it our duty to come from Madison to tell you that we consider your position precarious."

Madison was the capital of the state. Hurry Up knew that. So the men were undoubtedly from the Conservation Department. Likely they were the heads of the forestry, law enforcement, and perhaps fisheries or some other division.

By now Hurry Up had sidled close enough to become a part of the group. He could see Ethereal through the screen door on the straight-back kitchen chair holding his sister Estelle.

"Let's put it this way," Goose Gait said. "Let's give it a few more days. Let's not just hurry off after hanging around this long. Maybe it'll rain. Maybe we'll be able to hold those fires. Our lives are here. We just can't abandon everything."

There was a murmur of assent from the others of the Bloody Burn Bay area, and then Hurry Up's father said: "And let's get back to work. We've wasted enough time here talking. We've got a telephone alarm system operating. We're leaving a truck at every home. If the fires do start traveling in this direction, I think everybody can get out."

The men began to drift back to their trucks, and the three men from the department back to the automobiles.

Hurry Up went around to the back of the house and put the fox kit in the box, and then, trying to act as though nothing at all had happened to him or the fox, returned to the house to get some milk.

His mother had put Estelle down and given her a bottle. Now she turned to him. "Harry, where have you been? You know I want you to eat breakfast. It's the most important meal of the day."

It was only then he discovered he was hungry. He ate two bowls of oatmeal and could have eaten more, but his

63

mother had already scraped the kettle, so he satisfied himself with an extra glass of milk. Then, pouring canned milk into a pan, he took it out to the fox.

When the fox had drunk the milk, he went back into the cottage to get two slices of bread. While he was feeding them to the fox, he heard Ethereal call: "Harry? Harry!"

He walked around to the front of the cottage. "Aren't you going to do your chores today?"

In the excitement he had forgotten them, but now he took the garbage to the far end of the clearing where next year's garden would be and buried it. Then he went to the house for the lard pail with the tight cover, and headed down the road to Ham Hocks' place because they kept three cows and sold milk. On the way he stopped at the mailbox and picked up the mail. There was only an advertisement and the Otter City Gazette.

He glanced at the front page. All the stories, it seemed, were about the forest fires, and about how the lack of tourism "in this summer of calamity might be the economic ruin of the north."

He didn't quite know what it meant, except he suspected it wasn't good. Back at the house he swept away the sand the men had tracked onto the front porch, and then he lugged thirty buckets of water from the Bay to the two rows of lettuce, the only green thing left in the burnt-out garden.

Coming for his last pail of water, he stretched out on

the dock to see if the muskie was still beneath it. The water looked bronze, and it was difficult to see. The longer he looked, the clearer it became, and finally he could see Spade Face by his piling, fins fanning as though in slow motion, jaws moving almost imperceptibly as the fish took in water to run over its gills for the oxygen.

After the last bucket was poured along the lettuce rows, he rested with the fox in his lap at the edge of the burned lawn beneath a leaning cedar, which instead of being green, had turned coppery like everything else.

It occurred to him now that it had been a somewhat difficult summer, with no visiting around because of the danger from the fire. Other summers he might go at least once to swim with the Loud Mouth Kids, or a time or two to play with Ham Hocks' two boys, but this summer everyone stayed strictly at home. Even his mother wasn't good company, for the threat of forest fires only served to increase her dislike of the north country.

He couldn't understand his mother's loneliness, but thought it was probably because he couldn't understand the life she had led as a little girl in Boston. There were no forests or lakes there, but streets running past houses which stood side by side in long rows. Hurry Up pitied anyone who would have to live in a house so crowded by others it seemed there was hardly room to breathe. As far as he was concerned there was no more wonderful place to be than in this north country with its tall trees, thousands of blue lakes and streams, and tens of thousands of birds and animals.

Except, of course, during a summer like this one had turned out to be. Then it jolted him that before long the summer would be gone, and he would be required to go back to school. Then he'd only have weekends to roam, but only after the chores were done—and sometimes they could be considerable.

He got up and wandered a little way back among the trees with the fox at his heels. A huge pine had gone down in the wind storm of three years ago, and he climbed the sloping trunk, straddling it like a horse. He looked up, wishing that he could see blue again instead of the film of white smoke, like thin gauze pulled layer upon layer over the sky.

The fox on the ground whined impatiently for him to come down. When he didn't, the kit put his forepaws on the leaning tree and tried to scramble up the trunk. But he always fell back, so, tiring of the effort, he wandered off into the underbrush. Hurry Up would have called to him, except it suddenly dawned on him that he hadn't even given the fox a name.

Well, he'd have to take care of that, and he wondered what it should be. Foxy? No, too kiddish. Red? Too common. Maybe he'd have to wait to see what name fitted—like Fish Fins never got his name until after he'd become a guide, and Sugar Plum wasn't named until people knew how tart she could be, and Bear Paw wasn't called Bear Paw until his hands had grown huge enough to warrant the name.

So Hurry Up just called: "Fox, come here. Here, Fox. Here."

Then, when he suddenly remembered the near disaster of the morning, he leaped from the leaning tree trunk and ran through the brush. The fox was standing beneath a small sugar maple tree and it had something in its mouth.

Hurry Up went over. It was a young red squirrel, eyes already open, and it was alive.

Well, that was good, Hurry Up thought, because the fox would have to learn to hunt. Instead of killing and eating the young squirrel, the fox dropped it, and then when it ran, pounced on it, picked it up and carried it awhile before dropping it again.

Hurry Up wished the fox would kill the squirrel. He was not squeamish. Hunting and killing were all parts of his life, but he could plainly see the little squirrel was beginning to suffer. There was this much in the code as handed down by his father: everything, if it had to die, at least deserved a quick and merciful death.

His father always set his muskrat, beaver and otter traps so that the animals would drown themselves almost instantly. He never failed on any day, no matter what the weather, to visit his trapline so no animal had to suffer through a second cold night. He would track a wounded deer until it was killed or the track was undoubtedly lost.

So Hurry Up took the red squirrel from the fox and held it in his hand and wondered what to do with it.

If only the fox would kill and eat the squirrel the lesson would be a valuable one. Perhaps the cruel play was all part of the catch and kill lesson, but Hurry Up decided that was too painful a process—for him and the squirrel.

He wondered where the squirrel nest was and began hunting through the surrounding trees and probing the pine stumps. When he could find no nest, he looked again at the tiny animal in his hand and thought perhaps the best thing was to kill it, because it was already dying.

"Why don't you kill it, Fox?" he asked. And the fox sat looking up at the squirrel, its sharp ears erect, its tiny, sharp face turning from side to side so it could view the victim from all angles.

"For a fox you're not very smart," the boy said. The fox whined as though impatient to get on with the game of plaguing the squirrel.

"Oh no, you don't," Hurry Up said.

The squirrel's eyes were blinking, its head nodding, and the tail which had been held stiffly erect began to droop.

"He's dying," Hurry Up said. "So I suppose I might as well kill him."

Then he thought of the muskie under the pier. "On second thought," he said to the fox, "I think I'll give him to the fish. That way he won't be wasted."

He started out of the forest and went around the house, keeping the red squirrel out of sight in his hand, because he knew his mother would disapprove of what he was doing. The little fox trailed along, leaping from time to time, as though to get the quarry he perhaps rightly considered his.

"You had your chance," Hurry Up said. "Next time you'll know enough to kill and eat it."

The boy believed the fox would learn a lesson at being deprived of his prey, and that the next time it caught a squirrel or other small animal, it would be more possessive. Next time it might kill its victim instantly and then run off to eat it in peace.

Bloody Burn Bay was bright and brassy as they came down the path to the dock. It didn't look like water, but like molten copper, and Hurry Up thought it seemed almost solid enough to walk on.

He didn't want to throw out the squirrel if the muskie wasn't under the pier, so he bent to look first. The little fox was all over him the moment he flattened out. He had to hold the squirrel far out in front, over the water, lest the fox get it.

Even then the fox was so bumptious that Hurry Up never did get a clear look, but he thought he saw the shadowy figure of the fish next to the piling.

By the time he got back up the squirrel was all but dead. He wondered, as he looked at it, if there was enough life in the squirrel to bring the muskie charging to the top. He knew full well that a muskellunge wouldn't take anything unless it was alive and kicking. But, perhaps when the squirrel hit the water, it would revive and squirm, and maybe kick enough to entice the fish to action.

But he must not throw it too far, he thought. If he did, and the squirrel didn't swim, the muskie might not see it. He picked a spot about ten feet out, and then moved his arm sideways to make the toss. When he did, the fox jumped into the air trying to grab the squirrel.

Using the same motion he used when skimming a rock, he gave the squirrel a toss. It sailed through the air and landed in the water. The fox ran to the edge of the pier and looked out at it. Then the fox's tiny hind paws came forward and he braced with his front feet. Before Hurry Up knew what the fox was up to, he had launched himself, hit the water, and begun paddling frantically to retrieve the squirrel.

But the squirrel must have already been dead when it hit the water, because it did not move, and the only waves on the water were in the V the fox was making as it swam.

At first Hurry Up was delighted at the fox's bravado. He knew that foxes, though they weren't frightened of water, had some of the tendencies of the cat and avoided it when possible.

But the pride he felt in his pet's accomplishment swiftly changed to horror.

Spade Face came out! He swam stealthily at first, and then, when he was below the animal, lifted with a swift, deadly thrust and grabbed at the soft underparts of the little swimming fox. The muskie sank his inch-long, razor-sharp teeth into the animal's belly. Then when he found that the fox was too large to be instantly pulled under, the fish shook it, as though to tear the fox into two pieces for easier handling.

Hurry Up stood frozen. He wanted to scream but couldn't. He wanted to jump to the fox's aid, but found he was immobilized. Only when the fox gave a sharp, bark-like scream did Hurry Up dive in and drive the muskie back to his lair.

But Hurry Up was too late. The little fox's intestines were floating like long, tiny balloons. Blood was streaking in all directions. The fox gasped only once, twice and a third time before laying his head over into the water. Then the body floated gently, moving up and down from the waves Hurry Up had made when he jumped.

SIX

Now Hurry Up knew what hate was. He discovered that it was not a thing of rage, but a slow, burning desire for revenge. He also knew now what sadness was. And he knew that it was not a thing of tears, but an empty, lonely time of looking out over Bloody Burn Bay and seeing nothing.

The little fox was buried now, down near the creek. His father, who had come home in time to help, had rolled a large stone over the grave. Then, when Hurry Up still hadn't wept, Harry Senior said: "I'll keep my eyes open for a puppy."

But Hurry Up had spun around and said, "I don't want a puppy!"

His mother picked some of the petunias she had been watering so faithfully right through all the drought, and handed them to Hurry Up for the grave. The boy took

them, but, when his mother went back into the house, he
threw them into the bushes.

For several days he never went near the pier. Instead
he walked into the forest and sat where Bittersweet
Creek ran over some rocks, because he knew if he
looked at the water long enough, it would induce a
mildly hypnotic spell. And he found it was more comfortable to be in a trance, much more comfortable than
to have to face up to a world without his fox.

But, of course, he was much too young and healthy to
be long content with such inaction. So, though his hate
did not dissolve, it changed into an active desire for
vengeance. He would kill Spade Face! Rip him open!
Throw his body on Stony Bar where a bear or an otter
or the birds could eat it.

His mind ticked off the ways in which vengeance
might be his, and the quickest and simplest way he could
think of was to take his fishing rod, tie on a surface lure,
and cast for the fish. Spade Face would strike the lure.
He would think it was another mouse swimming, or a
frog—or the fox.

When he went to the house for the rod, his mother
asked: "Going after the muskie?"

Harry turned on her belligerently, lower lip thrust out.
But there was nothing of disapproval on her face, so the
short hairs at the nape of his neck smoothed down, and
he merely said: "Yes."

Ethereal reached for him then, but when her hand

touched his shoulder, she didn't close the fingers, but merely let the hand lie there. Then she asked: "To eat? Or only to kill?"

Hurry Up couldn't answer, so he turned away, and her hand slid from his shoulder.

When he was back outside he first realized he was breathing hard, as though he had been running. He felt trickles of sweat on both cheeks, felt the wetness of sweat in the palms of his hands.

He looked up as though the sun might have the answer, but it was only an indistinct, white blob in back of the smoky haze which held Bloody Burn Bay—and the world.

Maybe it was the terrible heat. Maybe it was the dryness—a dryness which made the shingles curl, the pier boards warp, the leaves become crisp, the grass turn to dust. Perhaps it wouldn't have been so necessary during a time of coolness, rain or even dew. Perhaps if the forests had been green instead of brown, bronze, brittle . . .

Hurry Up shook himself. The idea that the weather, the fires, might in some way be to blame was not original with him. He had heard his father blame the weather for the quarrels his parents were having.

"You always think of Boston," Harry Senior had said, "when the snow is too deep or the sun is too hot or the wind too cold. You don't mean to tell me they never have bad weather back in Boston?"

Except that right now Hurry Up couldn't have cared whether they quarreled when the weather was good or bad. Right now he'd be willing to go to Boston, or any other place to live, except he had to do this thing first.

He went around the house into the shed where any number of fishing lures were hanging on a two-by-four. One was shaped and colored like a mouse. It even had beady, glass eyes and a long, black trailing tail.

He took the imitation mouse down and put it on the edge of the box which had, for a brief time, been the home of the fox. Then he threaded the line from the reel up through the rod guides, and from the two-by-four took a metal leader and tied it to the end of the line.

He reached for the imitation mouse, turned it with his fingers to look it over, and then tested each of the nine hooks which hung in gangs of three to see if they were sharp. Then he undid the snap on the leader, and, hooking on the lure, closed it. He held the rod in one hand and walked toward the pier, being careful to hold the mouse by its tiny tail so the hooks wouldn't become fastened in his overalls.

He positioned himself on the first two shore boards of the pier so the muskie would not see his shadow on the water. With both hands on the rod, he cast diagonally. The little imitation mouse which someone—perhaps Fish Fins Larrens—had carved from a piece of balsa wood, hit the water with a soft splat.

The treble hooks beneath gave it stability, and it rode

the water like a real live mouse. Its beady, black eyes shined even at a distance, and its long tail of black fish string trailed out behind.

Hurry Up lowered the rod tip, and then began to slowly turn the reel handle. The mouse came toward him cutting a V in the water. He twitched the rod tip ever so slightly to give the mouse the uncertain momentum some land animals exhibit when forced to swim for the first time.

He was braced for the strike, because he meant to strike back and sink the hooks so deep that no amount of jumping on the part of the muskie would dislodge them.

Ethereal had come to the cottage door and was watching, though he didn't know it. She stood with one hand braced against the door jamb, and with the other she held back the screen door.

The little, brown, mouse-like lure was halfway back to the pier when out of the corner of his eye Hurry Up saw the fish rise like a blur of green lightning. In his eagerness he almost struck too quickly. If he had, he would have lofted the lure right out of the water, taken it away from the muskie.

But he made himself wait, hold steady until the water boiled and the mouse disappeared. Then he reeled line swiftly, and at the same time threw his entire body into setting the hooks.

Instantly the muskie vaulted clear of the water, his

mouth agape and the red gills glistening and the white teeth shining and the great head writhing from side to side to rid itself of the hooks which had pierced the cartilage of his jaw.

Hurry Up had the urge to end it right then and there by using all his strength and yanking the muskie out onto the pier so that he could haul him ashore and bash in his head with a rock. But he had thought it out, and he knew that to put too much pressure on the rod or on the line might be disastrous. The rod or the line might break, or the hooks might pull out.

So he meant to tire the fish, wear him down—fight him until he turned on his back and showed his white belly as a sign of defeat.

He had done all this thinking before casting. Now there was only time to keep a tight line. The muskie vaulted into the air three more times—high, like a long, green bird without wings.

Then, when it couldn't dislodge the imitation mouse, the fish ran for deeper water. Hurry Up kept the pressure on, but he didn't try to stop the fish. Far out the fish stopped. Then Hurry Up began to take back line, a little at a time.

Gradually he worked Spade Face back to the pier, but when he took a step forward to be in a better position for landing, the muskie saw him and at once headed again for deeper water. So Hurry Up had to repeat the process and stop the fish's run by gradually increasing friction on the reel spool with his thumb. When Spade Face stopped running, he turned him and began cranking the reel again.

The boy was streaked with sweat by the time the fish was alongside. His overalls had darkened with the moisture.

Ethereal still stood watching. But she had stepped out of the doorway onto the porch. She stood with one hand to her mouth as if to keep herself from screaming.

Hurry Up was completely absorbed in catching Spade Face. This time when the muskie came alongside the pier, he lay on his side, fins waving feebly, tail undulating like a leaf which is dead and about ready to fall from the tree.

Hurry Up got to his knees so he'd be in a position to get a hand beneath the muskie's gill covers. He held the rod high, and the fish rolled all the way over showing his white belly.

Now is the time, the boy thought. Now he is whipped, and now I must land him. Now he knows how it feels to be helpless. Now he's mine.

Hurry Up reached down, and his fingers slid along the white belly upward to where he could get a grip under the gill covers. But the instant the boy's fingers touched Spade Face, the fish flipped over and dived.

Hurry Up jumped back to his feet to keep the line tight. Then he tried to reel the muskie back to the surface, but it felt as though his line was tied to the bottom of Bloody Burn Bay. He could not retrieve it. He pulled until the rod was bent into a bow, and then he knelt and bent and looked under the pier.

Spade Face was there. He had wrapped the line around a piling which held the pier up. When the fish saw the boy's head come over the side of the pier, he gave a thrust with his tail, and the line snapped.

Spade Face lay still for a moment as though not realizing he was free. Then slowly he began to swim off, the imitation mouse still hanging to his jaws. He was trailing the wire leader and about two feet of fish line.

Hurry Up sat down exhausted, and Ethereal came running, because she felt sure that now the tears would come. But Hurry Up was not crying. There were tears. She could see that. They were just back of his eyes, shining to come out. But he didn't let them spill, and so there was nothing to say, except: "Too bad, Harry. Too bad. But you almost had him, and now maybe he'll go away and never come back."

Hurry Up hadn't thought of that. It was bad enough, the fish getting away. But to go off somewhere, to be forever out of his reach. That was something he hadn't contemplated.

"I'll get him," the boy said savagely. "I'll get him!"

Ethereal's hand was back over her mouth. She was so confused by her son that she didn't know what to say, how to talk to him. It was all part of this savage north country, she thought. It is all part of being too cold or too hot and forever running barefoot or wearing high boots.

But she stifled her antagonism and searched for some words which might comfort her son. All she could think to say was: "Harry, I've made some lemonade. Why don't you come up to the house and have a glass?"

She went up the dust path to the cottage, and Hurry Up sat for a while not moving. Finally he got up slowly, and reeled in the slack line. Then he turned and followed on up to the house.

He braced the rod beside the door and went in. The lemonade was already poured, so he took a glass, but he did not sit down with his mother. Instead he went outside and walked a little way into the forest where he could sit with his back to a tree. The lemonade was getting warm by the time he began to sip it.

Twice that afternoon he went down to the pier to lie flat on his stomach, peering over the edge to see if Spade Face had come back. But there was no sign of the muskie.

The fish would get rid of the lure. Hurry Up was certain of that. Spade Face would rub his snout into the gravel again and again until the hooks wore such large holes in the jaw cartilage that the mouse would drop off.

He wasn't sure whether or not the muskie would come back, but he thought he might. He knew that muskies, having laid claim to a lair, didn't like to leave it, and he had heard often how muskie hunters had seen the same fish time and again on the same bar even though they'd been hooked once and sometimes several times.

The pier was not only a good lair, but so dim and cool that perhaps nowhere in Bloody Burn Bay was there a better place for a big fish to hide out. And it concealed the big muskie so well that all those small fishes coming to the shade, never knew that green death in the form of a sleek muskie waited in the shadows.

Harry Senior came home that night for a change of clothes and a basket of supplies. Ethereal told him about the boy and the muskie when they were alone, so the father went out into the evening seeking his son, and found him resting under a hemlock.

"I hear you almost got that muskie that killed your fox." Harry Senior had brought it right out into the open, which was like him, but it surprised Hurry Up.

"Almost," Hurry Up said.

"What happened?"

"Snagged around a post."

"Break the line?"

The boy nodded.

"Well, if he doesn't come back you can forget him. Right?"

The boy didn't answer.

"Oh, come on now, Hurry Up." He always called him Hurry Up when Ethereal wasn't around. If she was present, it was Harry.

Still the boy was silent.

"You know," Harry Senior said, "you're making a big thing out of nothing."

It was the wrong thing to say. The boy jumped to his feet. "Nothing! What do you mean, nothing?"

"Well, what I mean is," Harry Senior stammered and then got on with it, "what I mean is, after all, it was only a fox and not, for instance, your sister, Estelle."

For a brief flashing moment Hurry Up was tempted to retort: "I wish it had been Estelle. Rather her than the fox."

But the enormity of such a breach of family faith hit him in time to keep him from saying it. But also, in that instant, he came to know that his father was too old to remember how a boy can love a young fox for a while even more than his sister or even his mother and father. And how he can have the capacity to hate a fish with all his energy right down to the deepest gut string in his body.

So he didn't say anything, except to end the discussion with a noncommital, "I suppose so."

Harry Senior shrugged. He couldn't help. Hurry Up was going to have to work this thing out himself.

That night the boy lay in bed looking down at the way his feet made a little tepee of the sheet. Even in the darkness it was so hot he felt sweat trickling down his rib cage. He wondered if the world would ever again be fresh and brisk and clean, and if the taste of smoke would go away, and whether the bite of smoke in his eyes might someday end.

Next morning after breakfast he was down at the pier on his stomach to see if the fish had come back.

When he went back into the house, Ethereal asked: "That muskie come back?"

Hurry Up shook his head.

"Isn't likely, then, that it will."

"He might. Soon as he gets the lure out of his jaws."

"And when's that likely to be?"

"Anytime. Within a day or two. They can do it."

"Well, for the muskie's sake, I hope he gets it out. It would be terrible to have to starve to death because of hooks in your mouth."

Hurry Up hadn't considered the possibility of the muskie starving. But now it worried him. Not because he felt sorry for the fish, but because if the fish starved he would never know it. If the fish died, he would always be waiting, and the need for revenge would stay inside him.

But the depression he had felt the preceding day had vanished. If he wasn't his old self, at least he was feeling better. He offered to dry the breakfast dishes, and asked before leaving the cottage: "Anything you want me to do, Mom?"

When she shook her head and told him to go play, he went down to the pier for another look, and then decided to walk up Bittersweet Creek. He went as far as the first

83

spring hole, which was just barely bubbling. Then he knelt and cupped his hands and brought up icy water and let it run over his face and neck. He drank some of the water and started back.

He had told himself he wouldn't go to see if the muskie was back until toward evening, but as soon as he was within sight of the pier, he knew he was going to look anyway.

He went down, lay on his stomach, and bent his head over. Then he waited, and at first when he saw the muskie he thought he was seeing things. Then he thought that perhaps it was another muskie that had come to lay claim to Spade Face's lair. So he lay until he could see more clearly.

Then he saw it. The lacerated jaw, a slender piece hanging, was white where the cartilage had been ripped away by the hooks.

It was Spade Face! The muskie had come back!

SEVEN

He went at once for the fishing rod, and tied on a new leader. Since there were no more imitation mice to hook on, he selected what he had heard Fish Fins call a yellow globe.

It was supposed to be a good muskie lure. It was a floater, with a silver flange just back of the head which revolved when it was retrieved. It was yellow with orange spots and about as long as a banana.

At the shore he stayed well back so the muskie could not see him. He cast diagonally again and retrieved the lure just swiftly enough so that the metal flange turned and flashes of silver light splintered from it.

But the muskie did not rise to the lure, so he lifted it and cast again. On the fifth cast the muskie came out, but he only swam behind the yellow globe as though inspecting it, and then sank back to the bottom and swam slowly beneath the pier.

When twelve casts produced no strikes, Hurry Up went back to the shed and, putting the yellow globe back on the two-by-four, took down a Skinner spoon. It was a long, wide spinner with treble hooks trailing. The hooks were camouflaged with feathers.

He went back to the pier and cast the spoon. Lights from the revolving spinner played like lightning through the water. The muskie came out with a rush. But inches from striking the lure, it stopped, and the boy could see the excitement shivering through the fish's fins, trembling through its whole body. The muskie did not open its jaws to close down on the feathered hooks. Instead, it backed off a little way. Hurry Up could see its malevolent eyes glaring, and he could see the torn jaw with its one hanging sliver of cartilage, and he could see the light flashes from the spoon glancing off the long, green body.

"Take it, Muskie," Hurry Up whispered. "Take it!"

But again the muskie sank to the bottom and swam to the shadows beneath the pier. Hurry Up cast the spoon twenty times before giving up. Then he went to the shed and brought down all the lures—some twenty—and tried each one, but the fish never came back out.

So Hurry Up lay on his stomach and hung his head over so he could look. The muskie was still there, just inches off the bottom. The long, jutting jaws moved almost imperceptibly as it took water into its mouth to pass under the gill covers.

Maybe a live frog, Hurry Up thought. Gathering up

the lures, he took them back to the shed, but instead of untangling one from the other, he put the tangle in the box for some other time when he wasn't faced with the problem of catching the muskie.

Then he went to the house to get a sock to carry the frogs, but his mother kept him for lunch. He ate swiftly and without relish. As quickly as he could leave the table, he excused himself, and, taking a sock, headed for the swamp hole.

Now the swamp pocket was almost dry. The green scum which had floated on the tepid water lay in dry, lifeless skeins on the cracked mud. Only at the very core of the pocket, a small place which thirsty animals had deepened by coming to drink, was there water.

Hurry Up got to his knees to scan the water surface and the surrounding clumps of browning cattails for the bug-eyes of the big frogs. He didn't see any.

He waded in. The water was only ankle deep. He felt around with his toes to see if, perhaps, any frogs had dived and were hiding from the heat by burying them-selves in the mud. But his toes only felt small stones, a stick, and one two-inch long mud minnow which tried so hard to escape it flipped itself out onto the caked mud.

It was much too small to be a bait for a fifteen pound muskie, so he toed it back into the water, and was about to turn away when he saw something. He bent, holding his breath. It was a frog, solemnly blinking to clear mud from its eyes.

He crouched, remembered that a frog can jump only forward, and then slowly brought his cupped hand in the direction the frog was facing. When there were six inches between his hand and the blinking amphibian, he pounced and almost squeezed the life right out of the frog, he held it so tightly.

Having but one frog, he didn't bother with the sock. He carried the bait by the hind legs, and loped for home.

In the shed he put the frog into the sock while he sat and made a fish string harness. He dangled a single, large hook from the harness, and tied it to the fish line. Then he reached into the sock and brought out the frog. He slipped the frog into the harness, pulled the slip knots tight, and there he had a live lure.

It was a large brown frog with green rims around its eyes. Its throat was throbbing in the heat, and its long hind legs sprawled out when Hurry Up set it on the shed floor. Lying there, it did not try to escape. It didn't even kick out when Hurry Up picked up the rod and lifted the frog by the harness off the floor.

Too hot, the boy thought. Too hot almost to think. Too hot for a frog to kick.

He started for the pier then, but detoured around the house, because he didn't want Ethereal to see how he'd harnessed the frog. She would say that he was cruel. She would never understand about such a thing.

When he came to the pier he sat to think about how he should employ the lure to best entice the muskie. He was afraid that if he cast too hard, the frog might slip from the harness. Perhaps if he just flipped the frog far enough so it would be within the muskie's line of vision.

No, that wouldn't do. He'd have to get it out far enough so if the frog swam toward the pier there would be plenty of time for the muskie to lift and to strike.

Maybe twenty feet. That wasn't much of a cast. He examined the harness, tested the lines which came around and under the frog's tiny forelegs. They seemed secure. He tested the line which held the hook behind the frog's rear legs. It was tight to the harness.

Well, what was he waiting for? He got up, let out enough line so that when he held the rod almost straight up, the frog dangled at eye level. Then he began to swing the frog back and forth. When he considered the momentum was about right, he gave the rod tip a flip and released his thumb from the line on the reel.

The frog went sailing. About twenty feet out it hit the water. But then instead of swimming, it lay quietly, back legs spread, little forearms straight down with every frog finger showing, and eyes bugging out of the water in the heat.

Hurry Up waited, but when the frog did not begin to swim, he moved the rod tip. The frog twitched. Ripples circled away from it. Still it did not move its legs. He tried again, and again. Then he tried to impart a swimming motion to the frog by moving his rod tip and taking up line on the reel each time he did.

He brought the frog all the way back to the pier, but the muskie did not show itself. He cast the frog again. This time he retrieved the frog in short, swift jerks. Once more, no luck.

The third time the frog was right alongside the pier and he was about to lift it from the water when the muskie hit. The strike came so close that water cascaded over the boy. When he opened his eyes, there was the frog harness dangling in front of him, but there was no frog in it. The muskie had grabbed the bait and yanked it right from the harness.

Hurry Up sank down on the pier. He raised the rod so that the harness came back to where he could put his fingers on it. It was intact. The hook was still there. The fish must have gotten a leg or a head hold and hit so hard the frog had been jerked free.

He lay down the rod, and then got to his stomach to look beneath the pier. When his eyes became accustomed to that dim place, the muskie came into focus. He was in his place by the piling, and Hurry Up felt the fish was staring at him with his evil eyes. He felt that the fish was daring him to try again. He felt now that the fish hated him as much as he hated the fish. And so, what had been simply a desire for revenge, turned into an obsession.

Now he would have to kill that muskie. There was no other way. He would have to find the fish's weakest spot and attack him there. He would have to destroy him.

But he didn't try anymore that day. It was enough

that his hate had hardened. He could live with it now that it was an obsession. It wasn't important now that the muskie die today or tomorrow or the next day. It was only important that he die. Hurry Up could choose his own time, he could take his obsession to bed with him, and he could dream of the muskie lying out there beneath the pier. He could even enjoy the dream because he told himself that in the end he would have the muskie's life.

But such a hate had to take its toll, and when morning came he was tired, and there were shadows under his eyes. The night had given him no plans for catching the muskie.

"You sure look peaked," his mother said, when he toyed with his milk, instead of drinking it. "You sleep all right?"

Hurry Up nodded. "I slept good," he said, but made no mention of the dreams.

"Well, you sure don't look it. You aren't letting that muskie get under your skin, now, are you?" she asked.

Hurry Up shook his head. Then, to avoid further questioning, he gulped his milk and, though he wanted to run, walked slowly and carefully through the door.

Once outside he headed for Bittersweet Creek. Of all places, it was the best to think. He found his favorite hemlock and crawled down to the coolest place, which was where the high water had gouged a cave beneath the curving roots.

How would an Indian get that muskie? he asked himself.

Well, he knew the reservation Indians used many methods. They were, of course, not subject to the same fish and game regulations the white man had to observe in pursuing his sport. On reservation lakes and rivers, the Indian might take fish by any method, and Hurry Up had even heard that some of them used dynamite.

Well, he wasn't ready yet to resort to dynamite, even though there was the usual supply of it in the shed for stump and rock removal, and, in the case of extreme emergency, for blasting out a fire break to contain a forest fire. Dynamite was dangerous. What's more, the explosion would bring the wrath of his parents crashing down around his ears.

Well, how else then? Indians netted and speared fish. Perhaps he could spear the muskie. There was a spear in the shed. His father used it sometimes in spring to spear suckers which ran the creeks. Sucker spearing was legal, because suckers, as opposed to game fishes, were considered rough fish.

But if Harry Senior ever found out he had speared the muskie, Hurry Up knew he would be in trouble. All fire tower watchers and fire fighters—most state men in the field—were also deputy game wardens. Though they didn't actively engage in seeking out fish and game regulation violaters, if they came across an offender, they were duty bound to arrest him.

92

He could hear his father now: "What a pretty kettle of fish! Here I am, and I'm supposed to arrest my own son for illegally spearing muskies. Harry Hanson Junior, whatever got into you? Have you lost your mind completely?"

Then if he yelled loud enough, it was likely that Ethereal would begin to cry. And with his father shouting, and his mother crying, Estelle would become upset and add her screams to the pandemonium.

Hurry Up stretched himself out so that his feet came out of the cave and were in the creek. The water was cool on his callouses. He wiggled his toes and poked them down into the fine silt along the slender stream of running water.

Of course, his father need never know. But there was Ethereal. She was always home, and if she saw him with a spear down around the pier, she'd certainly tell Harry Senior.

Fish and game regulation violations just weren't tolerated. Violating the fish and game laws was as bad as stealing in the eyes of the Bloody Burn Bay area people. Everyone would, of course, hear about it. He'd have a hard time facing up—even if he explained about how the fox had been killed by the muskie.

Hook and line. That was fair. Spear or net or dynamite. That was unfair. Illegal.

The helplessness of his situation, the hopelessness of it, almost overwhelmed him.

What if, he thought, instead of a fox kit the muskie had killed a baby? How then would Harry Senior and the people of the Bloody Burn Bay area have felt? Would they have resorted to every means at their disposal— illegal or not—to catch and kill that muskie? He knew they would. And, Hurry Up reasoned, wasn't that little fox just as important to him as some kid would be to his parents.

But, of course, parents would have a way of explaining such things, so that when you tried to answer them, you would suddenly discover you had no answers. Or, if you did, people would say they were all the wrong answers.

Even so, Hurry Up thought, adults sometimes twisted the law to suit themselves. Take bears, for instance. They were legal quarry only during the deer season. But just let a bear raid someone's bee hives! The warden would be there fast with steel traps, and, having declared the animal a public nuisance, he would proceed to catch and shoot it.

Or what about a mink that had raided someone's hen house in summer? The pelt would be no good that early, and the season on mink wouldn't open until November, but it wouldn't take the chicken farmer long to get permission to trap and kill the mink.

The state even paid a farmer for damage done to his crops by deer. But who was going to pay him for the fox? And who was going to give him permission to kill the muskie that had killed the fox? Were chickens or honey or apple orchards or corn fields any more important to their owners than the fox had been to him?

Of course, adults would say that honey or chickens were more important than the fox, but that was because they had forgotten how important a pet can be. The whole world was that way, Hurry Up thought. Parents made the laws, and they were fashioned for adults and didn't take into consideration such rights as a child thought important.

Well, Hurry Up wasn't just going to lie there and take it. He sat bolt upright, siezed by the sudden determination that, law or no law, he was going to get that muskie. And, if he couldn't spear him during the day when his mother would likely see him, he'd spear the fish at night.

Once resolved, the anger he felt for the governing generation dissolved. He got up and went to the spring hole to douse his head in the cold water. He put his face into the spring, and the icy water felt good against his hot, tired eyelids.

It seemed these days that his eyes and nose were always watering. Everybody was going around with red-rimmed eyes, because the air was never clear of smoke and the heat never abated. So a boy rubbed his eyes until they were so sore they felt as if someone had thrown sand into them.

When he couldn't hold his breath any longer, he lifted his head from the spring and started for home.

95

In the shed he found a pinch bar, and going to the pier he lay belly down and looked at the fish to mark the exact spot where he lay. Then he put the bar beneath a board and began to lever it up. The nails screeched and the board lifted. Then he went and loosed the other end of the board.

He put the board aside and lay on his stomach to peer through the opening. The muskie was directly below in approximately six feet of water. He took the nails out of the board and carefully replaced it. Then he took the pinch bar back and, getting out the spear, took a file from the work bench and began sharpening the four tines.

It was a long spear, with a pole of ten feet, and it had an overall spearhead spread of ten inches. He sharpened the prong tips until they shone. Then he put the file away and laid the spear down near the door so he could easily find it in the dark.

But the thought of what he was about to do frightened him now, and it must have been evident because at supper Ethereal asked what was bothering him.

"Just the heat," he said. It was a handy way of avoiding further questioning.

After supper he went outside and sat with his back to the bottom step of the porch. Ethereal came out with Estelle in her arms, and then while she sat in the rocker the baby stood beside her and tried to walk. Falling, she'd crawl back to the rocker and lift herself.

"Won't be long and she'll be walking," Ethereal said.

"Sure looks like it," Hurry Up agreed.

"If it would only rain," Ethereal said, wiping her brow with a handkerchief. "Seems like it hasn't rained for years and years. What a blessing rain is. I'll never complain again when it rains. Not if it rains for two weeks without stopping."

The mood rubbed off on Hurry Up. The heat seemed more oppressive, and it seemed he couldn't remember how rain felt when it hit a fellow's face. What a wonderful thing, he thought—rain on your face. Wet rain. Refreshing rain. Softening the ground. Closing the cracks in the earth. Filling the swamp pockets. Making the creek flow full and fast again. Washing the dust from the leaves, the smoke out of the air. Wetting down the forest fires. Putting them out.

"Gee I hope it rains soon," Hurry Up said, and it was almost a prayer, and then Ethereal said:

"So do I hope it rains, Harry. So do I, because no summer has been so dreadful. I've never been so afraid. I've never come to hate a place so much. God, Harry, but I hope it rains. Lord, how I hope that it does."

Then she got up and picked up Estelle because it was time to give her a bottle and put her to bed. But Hurry Up stayed on the porch, and he hardly noticed that it got dark, because the days were so dim that night just sort of crept up without any warning.

He went to bed at the usual time, but the thought of

what he planned to do kept him awake. He heard the clock strike nine-thirty, and then ten o'clock. He got up and sat on the floor by the window, but it was too dark to see the lake. He sat there until he heard the clock strike eleven, and then he got back in bed. When the clock struck twelve, he got up and pulled on his overalls.

He went down the stairs, carefully skipping the two steps which creaked, and, gliding through the kitchen, slipped out the door. Then he waited on the porch, listening. When there was no sound from his mother's bedroom he took the flashlight out of his back pocket and went out onto the lawn.

Still he did not light the light, but went in the dark around the house to where the shed loomed. He got to his knees and felt around on the ground for the spear. Lifting it, he balanced it in his left hand and walked slowly and quietly down to the dock.

Again he waited to see if there were any sounds from the house. When there was nothing he put the heavy spear down, removed the board, and then lying on his belly turned on the light and held the head of the flashlight close to the water. The fish was there. The light did not frighten it. Hurry Up was fascinated.

Hurry Up picked up the spear and, standing over the hole, aimed the spearhead down toward the fish. With the spear in one hand and the flashlight in the other, he stood poised, waiting for the fish to come into focus.

The flashlight made a bright spot on the water and reflected light back into his eyes, so he crouched. When he did, the outlines of the fish came into view. Carefully he put the spearhead into the water, and then he began to lower it.

His plan was to get the spearhead within two feet of the muskie before making his thrust. He would have to put all his weight into the thrust if he hoped to get the spear points through the scales which overlapped like armor plating.

Down the spearhead went, closer and closer. It was like peering down a steep cliff, and the weight of the spear and the beam of light bending off in the water gave him a feeling of falling. Then suddenly his balance was destroyed. He started tipping forward, and in an effort to catch himself he dropped the flashlight.

He heard it splash, and then he was on his hands and knees and the spear was caught at an angle between the boards. Carefully he retrieved the spear and laid it on the pier, but the flashlight was on the bottom of the bay. It was still lighted, and he could see it shining down there. A school of curious minnows swam into the circle of light. The muskie was gone.

EIGHT

Hurry Up wasted little time on breakfast the next morning, and as soon as it was over went down to the pier. The muskie was there, and the flashlight was lying beside the fish, but it had gone out. He put the pier board back in place but did not nail it down. Then, just as he was contemplating other ways of eliminating Spade Face, trucks began to arrive in the yard.

Goose Gait Goetz and his wife came first, followed by the widow, Sugar Plum, in a Model T Ford with a wide box where the back seat had once been. Then there was Mrs. Bear Paw Svendson and Mrs. Ham Hocks Garrity. Goose Gait waited around while the other women— Mrs. Weasel McGlint, Mrs. Fish Fins Larrens, Mrs. Siren Click—arrived, and then he left to battle fires on whichever front the men were fighting that day.

All the kids came along too—the Loud Mouth Kids (belonging to High Pockets Forsythe), and the Four Toes Gregory twins, all five of the Lane kids along with Mrs. Little Leak—until at last the yard was crawling with people.

Even Mrs. Shoot First Canuck's wife was there, so huge now with child that she reached out for things to hold onto when she walked. Mr. High Pocket Forsythe's wife, Pee Wee, made it a point of taking care of Mrs. Shoot First. She found a place for her in the shade, and, spreading a blanket, helped her ease down to a sitting position.

Last to arrive, and the only man at the gathering, was the preacher, High Heavens Winterspoon.

All the women put down shawls or blankets to sit on, because the grass on the front lawn had long been dead, and now there was only sand. And the kids were rounded up and made to sit in a huddle where they could be contained and kept quiet. Then High Heavens motioned for silence.

When the voices dwindled, and only Estelle in Ethereal's arms continued to whine a little, High Heavens began: "I'm sure most of you know by this time why we've come together. But if some of you haven't heard, let me tell you.

"The fires have joined and are about to encircle us. We are virtually in a trap. There are four roads still open to the outside, but even with a little wind, the fire would

101

spread so swiftly they would almost immediately be closed.

"I've made the rounds and talked to all the men. They think we ought to get out, evacuate, move to Otter City, and . . ."

There was an immediate murmur of dissent. It started like a little wind and then grew to a cyclone of sound.

High Heavens put up his hands for silence. "Let me finish," he shouted. "Hear me out!"

The crowd of children, taking advantage of the outburst, began to fragment. Sitting still on a scorching hot day was a difficult requirement, especially for the very young. So some broke away from the main huddle and added their voices to the clamor.

Mrs. Bear Paw Svendson got to her feet to help High Heavens restore order. She lifted her voice and got three times the volume High Heavens could command.

"Ladies! Ladies!" she bellowed, and the women quieted. "Children! Children!" And the youngsters stopped playing to look her way.

"Now if everyone will sit back down and be quiet and polite enough to hear Reverend High Heavens out, maybe we'll find out what he's got to say!"

There was something about Mrs. Bear Paw which commanded obedience. A tremendous hulk of a woman, she towered over all the others. So the women quieted. The children were drawn back into their huddle, and

High Heavens nodded his approval to Mrs. Bear Paw, even though he did it with a little lilt of his head as though he could have done as well if he had wanted to be so undignified as to shout as loudly as she had.

"Now the point is this," Reverend High Heavens went on in a more confident tone: "If we go now we'll have the chance to take many of our priceless possessions with us. If we wait, and the fire closes in, it will literally be a race with death, and there'll be no chance to take anything."

Mrs. Little Leak raised her hand. When it looked as though High Heavens was going to ignore her, she waggled it and shouted: "Reverend!"

So High Heavens, with a nod, gave her permission to speak and she said: "It would take a moving van to take all my beautiful furniture, my china, my rugs—what you call my 'priceless possessions'—with me. There aren't trucks in any of this north country big enough to haul everything out."

A murmur of assent went through the crowd. High Heavens held up both hands for silence. "Well, I wasn't exactly thinking of moving all your household things. I was only thinking of taking perhaps a few things which you valued most above everything else—like family heirlooms or mementos of your wedding day or a christening or a baptism—personal, intimate things."

"I'd rather stay right here and die in the fire than leave

my dining room set behind," Mrs. Fish Fins shouted. "Why we've only just got it paid for. We'd never get another!"

Another murmur of assent ran through the assembled women, and there were sympathetic undertones among the huddled children as perhaps one thought of a bicycle, a boat, or a wagon. And then one youngster wailed: "What about my dog?"

High Heavens waved for silence, but he didn't get it until Mrs. Bear Paw once again came to his assistance. "But what other choice have we?" the preacher asked. "I don't think this is the time to think of material possessions. I think this is the time to think of saving our lives and the lives of our children."

High Heavens knew he had made a telling point when he spoke of the children's safety. The silence was absolute as every woman thought about her own children, and how it would be for them if they were trapped.

High Heavens was about to resume and take advantage of the response he had finally evoked when there was a loud thump, a scream and a splash. All eyes turned toward Bloody Burn Bay, and there was one of the Gregory twins wedged in the pier, half in and half out of the water.

No one had seen the youngster slip away, and only Hurry Up giggled, because he knew the twin had stepped on the loose board, and it had flipped and the girl had gone through to her belly button.

That'll teach her to go nosing around, Hurry Up thought. And then his giggle erupted in laughter because only a fat stomach had kept her from going right on through.

It took fifteen minutes to pry the Gregory twin free, and to get the kids all huddled together again, and to quiet the women down.

When it was quiet, and High Heavens was once again ready to proceed, a heat bug hit a high note right in the tree beneath which the Reverend was standing.

High Heavens, mouth already open to speak, left it that way and stared up as though with only the force of his mind he could command the cicada to silence. But the insect went on shrilling, and High Heaven's face turned red, especially when he saw the smiles on the faces of some of the women watching him.

Finally, when the cicada showed no signs of shutting up, High Heavens took on a big, double lungful of air and let go: "And now," he shouted, "if we may continue. We are not unlike families who live on some river bottom and who, having been warned about an approaching flood, do not flee from it. We are not in a position to do what we'd like to do. We are only in a position to do what we have to do."

Most of the women couldn't hear him. So the Widow Sugar Plum raised a hand and waggled it, and it was as if her voice was what the cicada had been wanting to hear, because it stopped shrilling.

"But perhaps the fire won't come," the Widow said. "Maybe it will rain. Maybe the men will hold the fire off. There are hundreds out there fighting it now."

High Heavens put a forefinger to his nose. He always did when he was perturbed and had no pat answer for a question which had been raised. Finally he admitted: "Well, of course, you could be right. But then, what would we lose even if we did retreat? We could come back, and everything would be just as we left it."

Mrs. Ham Hocks Garrity put up a hand. The Reverend nodded in her direction. "What about the animals? We've got two cows."

Before he could answer, Mrs. Fish Fins had her hand up. "Where would we stay in Otter City? I have no relatives there."

Again there was a murmur of assent from the women. High Heavens signaled for silence. "I was coming to that," he said. "Arrangements have been made to stay at the Fair Grounds."

A half-dozen women echoed him: "At the Fair Grounds!"

He held up his hands and continued: "Yes, at the Fair Grounds. In the animal exhibit building."

"You mean in the horse stalls and the calf pens!" It was Mrs. High Pockets. Her voice was shrill. It was indignant.

"They'll be scrubbed out before you move in," High Heavens explained.

A loud wave of sound passed through the group, and then Mrs. Goose Gait got to her feet and, pointing a finger at Reverend High Heavens, asked: "You ever try to clean out a horse or a cow barn? You ever put water down on a floor that has known nothing except manure from the day it was laid?"

She waited, and when High Heavens saw that everyone waited for his answer, he only shook his head.

"Well, I'll tell you," Mrs. Goose Gait continued. "Water doesn't wash away. Water brings out the smells. And the more you wash, the worse it becomes. That odor is in there. The boards are soaked with it. You can make it worse by wetting it, but you can never get it out. And I for one don't aim to sleep in a pig pen!"

The women chorused their agreement. Reverend High Heavens held up both hands for silence. But the women were a long time in quieting. When there was but a rustle of voices, the Reverend said: "But, my dear ladies, we're talking about saving lives, so how can such a small inconvenience as an odor be a deterrent to doing what is best for all concerned?"

But obviously, Reverend High Heaven, who was a bachelor, knew nothing about women.

Finally Mrs. Fish Fins made herself heard above the noise of the crowd. "Are you going to Otter City?" she asked the preacher.

"Well, no, my place is with the men on the fire line," he said.

107

"Then maybe that's where our place is," Widow Sugar Plum shouted, even though she didn't have a man on the fire line.

The Reverend held up his hands, but Mrs. Bear Paw had to help. "Let's be polite, ladies. Let's be polite."

When it was quiet again, High Heavens said: "But your men want you out of here. They sent me here to get you. They're worried about you. Now if a man is truly the master of his house, then I'm surprised that you ladies don't concede that leaving here is the thing to do—obey your men."

If High Heavens had thought to score with that line of reasoning, he didn't know his women. These north woods women might concede that in theory the man was the head of the house, but their men were so seldom home that any household which depended on a man to run it would fold up instantly. Out here in the Bloody Burn Bay area, with men always off somewhere doing their jobs, women did everything from milking cows, if there were some, to shooting a bear if one came prowling.

Hurry Up, by now thoroughly bored with the whole proceedings, had edged his way to the outside fringe of the huddle of kids and was considering making a sneak for it. It was too hot for one thing, and the other children annoyed him with their restless scratching, yawning and fidgeting. If he could make it to where the buck-brush skirted the clearing, he wouldn't have any trouble getting to Bittersweet Creek, and then he could go to his cave and soak his head in the spring to cool off.

So he edged farther and farther from the gathering of children, but then all at once he felt eyes on him. They were, of course, Ethereal's, and it was just as though she had anticipated he might be ready to make a break for it. So there was nothing for him to do, except lie back on the hot ground, find a small stick, and draw pictures in the sand.

Reverend High Heavens had obviously come to a dead end. He didn't know what to say. If the women wouldn't leave, there was nothing he could do to make them.

"Listen, ladies," he said. "Listen," he repeated, waving his hands. The women quieted. "Now I want you to talk it over. Just remember what could happen if the escape routes were cut off and a wind came up. Think about everything I've said and talk it over. Then we'll take a vote."

He walked toward the house. Ethereal, with Estelle over one arm, followed. On the porch he sat in the rocker and mopped his forehead with a huge, blue handkerchief.

"Can I get you a drink, Reverend Winterspoon?" she asked.

"That would be nice," he said. She opened the screen door and was back shortly with a tall glass of lemonade. Moisture was already beading on the glass, and she took her apron to dry it before handing it to the preacher.

"I think you're right, Reverend Winterspoon," she said. "I think we ought to get out of here."

"Well, I hope the rest do," he said, sipping the cool drink.

"I hope so too."

He drank deeply then, and handed the glass back to her. "Of course," he said, "even if the others won't go, you can leave. There's no need for you to stay."

"Oh no," Ethereal shook her head. "If the others stay, then I stay. I'm part of the team. It's my job to see that Mrs. Canuck gets out safely. You know, the baby is due any day now. I couldn't go if the others stayed."

That was the way it had been planned, of course. They were to go out in teams. Each family was to travel with one other family. In that way no one would inadvertently be left behind.

"I suppose you're right," High Heavens said. "If the others elect to stay, I suppose it is your duty to stay with them. But I think they should get out."

"Maybe it will rain. It must pretty soon. How long is it since we've had rain? Three months?"

"Four months, not counting that one tiny shower in May," High Heavens said.

"Well, it can't go on much longer without raining. Can it?" Ethereal asked.

"It doesn't seem like it could. It would seem it just has to rain. It would seem that it can't hold off much longer."

Estelle whimpered, and Ethereal put her on the porch so she could crawl. The baby was down off the steps in an instant and crawling across the yard. Ethereal had to retrieve her.

"My goodness," she said, "it seems they're hardly born before they're trying to go off somewhere."

High Heavens nodded. Then he said: "Well, I suppose we'd better get back to the others."

High Heavens went ahead. Ethereal followed. The women had obviously said all they intended to on the subject, and were quiet now as they looked to the preacher.

He took his place within the semicircle and, after again mopping his face with his handkerchief, said: "Well, I suppose we can take a vote. But first I'd like to say that if we decide to stay, those who want to leave may. But they should make their intentions clear right now, so that we can make new evacuation plans."

Most of the women nodded, and Reverend High Heavens could see by the set expressions on their faces that the vote would be but a formality. But he had to go through with it now, so he said: "All those in favor of getting out put up a hand." Ethereal started to raise hers but, when no one else did, she kept it down.

If High Heavens was disappointed, it did not show on his face. Instead there was just the hint of a smile, perhaps because he was secretly pleased to see such an exhibition of bravery.

Not that he had ever been one to sell a north woods woman short. He knew the sacrifices many made so that their men could follow their chosen professions of fire fighters, tower watchers, loggers, guides, timber cruisers, and pulp cutters.

"All right," he said, "now let's see the hands of those who want to stay." Every hand went high—even Ethereal's—and the excitement of it ran in a ripple of laughter through the women, infecting the children who began to break out of their huddle and romp about.

"Now wait! Now wait!" High Heavens was shouting. But he would never have made himself heard if Mrs. Bear Paw hadn't risen to the occasion and thundered: "Now you kids settle back down. The Reverend isn't through talking. Just get back there. All of you. Back on the ground. You over there. I mean it. Get down and keep quiet!"

Order was restored. The children's voices simmered softly like bubbling soup. Then it was quiet.

"There's one more thing. Keep the telephone lines clear for emergencies. And the new disaster signal is three long rings. When you hear it, don't answer the phone. Just get into your truck and get moving.

"And remember," he cautioned, "to lift the receiver of your phone every half-hour to make sure that it's working, that the fire hasn't cut the lines. And keep food and water ready in the trucks, and see to it that the trucks have plenty of gas. And throw in some buckets so you can wet yourself down if need be. Put in blankets. Put shawls and handkerchiefs over your heads and faces.

"And last, but not least," he concluded, "make certain your children do not roam far from the house. Keep them within calling distance so that at the last minute you do not have to go into the woods to find a child.

"And now, let's say a prayer . . ."

At the mention of children, Ethereal raised up to see if Hurry Up was still with the group. But he had gone and, while she scanned faces searching for him, was walking along the banks of Bittersweet Creek.

He went straight to the spring and doused his head with icy water. Then he lay at full length in the slender trickle of water which was the creek. When he was soaked and cool, he got up and went to his cave beneath the roots of the huge hemlock.

For him there was no fear of fire. For him there was only the annoyance of being hot and sweating, of breathing through already raw nostrils, and looking out through red rimmed eyes at a hazy, smoky world from which the sun had all but disappeared and at a night sky in which the stars seldom shone.

For him the fire was only a vague nuisance, but the muskie was all too real. He could deal with the fire. He was sure of that. But how did you deal with a muskie? What could he do to get his revenge? To even the score? To kill the big fish which had killed his fox pup—his first real pet?

NINE

Next morning, first thing on rising, Ethereal checked with the telephone operator. "No the fires haven't advanced. The men are keeping them in check," the operator said.

"Well, that's good," Ethereal said. "I've got to run to Twin Forks to the grocery and to get some ice. I'm about out of things. And I want to check on Mrs. Canuck. She didn't look too well yesterday."

The telephone operator, a spinster, Miss Ring Me (Olivia) Huntington, said: "Well, have someone guard the phone. You've got a boy, don't you? Have him stay by the telephone."

Ethereal hung up and went to the door to call Hurry Up. The boy was down at the pier hanging over the edge looking down at Spade Face. When he came up, she said: "I've got to go grocery shopping, so you stay close to the telephone. Three long rings means we've got to leave. If you hear it, wait. I'll be right back. But don't answer. Not on three long rings. But if it's our ring, two long and two short, then you answer and see who it is."

Hurry Up nodded. It would put a crimp in his plans, but what could he do?

Ethereal put Estelle on the truck seat, and braced a board kept in the cab so she wouldn't slide off. Before she drove out, she cautioned Hurry Up: "Now, Harry, you mind me. Stay where you can hear that phone!"

So Hurry Up plumped down into the rocker on the porch and amused himself by pushing a toe in the way of an ant that wanted to cross over. The ant finally found a crack which the heat had widened and went beneath the boy's bare foot to escape.

Hurry Up had the urge to get a small stick and pry it from its runway, and then make it start all over again, but it didn't seem worth the effort.

This was going to be a wasted morning. He had been planning on somehow retrieving the flashlight before any-one noticed it was gone. He didn't want to dive down, because he didn't want to scare Spade Face. He wanted that fish where he was. As long as the muskie didn't move, Hurry Up was certain that, just as it would some day rain, he'd get Spade Face.

In fact now, with Ethereal gone, would be the ideal time to try the spear. He wondered if he could hear the telephone if he was as far away as the pier. He tried to remember. Had he ever heard it ring when he was down there? It seemed he had. He looked down at the pier, judging the distance. Would the shrill ringing of the telephone carry that far? He guessed it would. But what if it wouldn't? And, what if the phone rang while he was down there?

But it shouldn't take him long. He could get the spear, hurry down there, spear the fish and then throw the body off somewhere into the buckbrush, and be back on the porch in ten minutes.

Still he had promised he'd stay on the porch. Or had he really? Hadn't he only promised to stay close enough to hear the telephone? He couldn't remember now just what it was he had promised.

Hurry Up got up and walked off the porch. He went halfway down to the pier and looked back at the cottage. He was sure he could hear the telephone from that distance. He went a little farther, and stopped to turn back again.

He wished the phone would ring so he could tell. Usually with a party line of eight homes it was always ringing. But in the emergency all unnecessary calls were prohibited, and the telephone was unusually quiet.

Hurry Up dug a toe into the sand. Sometimes that helped him to think.

The operator had said the men were holding their own against the fires. She had said it hardly more than an hour ago. He had heard Ethereal talking to Miss Ring

Me. So how could the situation have changed within the hour? If the men were holding back the fires an hour ago, they would be holding back the fires now.

He turned toward the pier and took a few more steps. He stopped, dug a toe into the sand. The telephone rang. He was so surprised he didn't believe it and missed the signal. His heart raced, and he was surprised to discover he was suddenly short of breath.

The phone rang again. Two long rings and two short. It was their ring. He dug his bare heels into the sand and raced for the cottage. He crossed the porch in two bounds and slammed through the screen door. When he lifted the receiver he was so out of breath he couldn't talk.

"Hello. Hello. Hello!" He recognized the voice. It was his father.

"It's me, Dad," he finally managed to say.

"Where's your mother?"

"Went to Twin Forks."

"Oh? Everything all right?"

Hurry Up had his breath back. "Sure, everything is fine here."

"Well, I just had to check. Everybody thinks the women should leave."

Hurry Up hesitated. "They didn't want to," he finally said. He could hear his father breathing.

"Well, just tell your mother I called," his father said.

"When are you coming home?" Hurry Up asked.

"I don't know. We've got a little trouble right now. So I don't know."

Hurry Up suddenly felt a terrible need to have his father come home. He couldn't explain why he should have this urgent need for his father's physical presence. After all, he was talking to him. "I wish it would end, Dad," he finally said.

"Wish what would end?" his father asked.

"The fires."

"Oh. Well, I wish they would end too. But there's no rain in the forecast."

"What do you think?" Now he wanted to hold his father on the line.

"I don't know, Son. I don't know. But we have to get off this telephone. Now be good." Neither of them said good-bye. When Hurry Up heard the receiver click at the other end of the line, he hung up.

He went back to the porch and sat in the rocker. If he had his fox things wouldn't seem so bad. That muskie! Man, what he wouldn't give to run a knife into that fish's belly and rip it wide open. Then it would know how it feels to be torn to pieces—the way it had torn the fox to pieces—and even before he'd had a chance to name it.

What would he have named the fox? Wrestler? Well, he was a pretty good one, but it wasn't, well . . . it didn't fit the animal. Maybe Copperking. He had been getting coppery, and Copperking had a pretty good ring to it. "Copperking," he tried it aloud. "Copperking."

He heard the truck before he saw it, and was down in the dust when it came around the curve where the white birch leaned almost across the road.

Ethereal looked red, and she was sweating. Estelle, braced by the wide board on the front seat, was howling her head off.

"What a country!" his mother exploded when she saw him, as though he was somehow responsible for the state of things. "And that poor woman down there!" She must have been talking about Mrs. Canuck who was going to have a baby.

"Take those groceries in," Ethereal said, motioning to a gunny sack in the back of the truck. Then with an ice tongs she lifted out a square of dripping ice. After the ice was in the ice box, she went back for the howling baby. Hurry Up shouldered the bag of groceries and, bending beneath the weight, followed her up the steps and into the house.

While she put the baby down and lighted the kerosene stove to warm a bottle, Ethereal talked: "I can tell you one thing for sure, Harry Hanson. I can tell you when this is all over that your father and I are going to have a talk. And I can also tell you that if he doesn't agree to go to Boston, you and Estelle and I are going, and he can stay right here in his north woods. I've had it! I have had it right up to here!" And she made a motion across her throat with her forefinger.

Hurry Up wanted to get away, so he edged toward the

door. "Oh no you don't! You just wait now, Mister Hanson! You just wait," his mother said. "You start helping around here, and you can begin by putting those groceries away. I think it's about time you helped around the house."

Hurry Up opened the gunny sack and began taking out bags and packages, jars and cans.

"And that's another thing," Ethereal said, pushing the pan in which the bottle was standing in to the back of the stove. "That's another thing," she repeated, picking up the bottle and trying a few drops of milk on her forearm. "Harry Senior says you're to do outside work. That you're not to do housework."

It was the first time Hurry Up had heard about it, but, now that his mother mentioned it, he realized that all his chores were done outdoors.

Ethereal stopped talking because the baby's wailing had gone an octave higher. Taking the bottle, she went over to where Estelle, naked except for a diaper, was lying in her crib. The baby reached for the bottle, and the howling subsided.

"I'm telling you, Harry Hanson Junior, this is no life for anyone," his mother went on when the house was quiet again. "Why I haven't been out of this house except to shop and go to church for four months! What kind of living do you think that is?"

Hurry Up wondered why she was talking to him like that. She had never done it before. It frightened him.

But she didn't stop. "If you could only see the house I was brought up in, the house where your grandmother and grandfather live. If you could see that big white house and the clean streets, and the big elms and the white sidewalks.

"Harry, it's cool there in the morning. It's cool there every morning. There's a freshness to the air. Not smoke, smoke, forever smoke!"

Ethereal sat in a chair at the kitchen table. She put her head down on her arms. Then she sobbed softly. Hurry Up felt tears rise to his eyes in sympathy. He didn't know what to say or do, and he was so confused he put the bars of soap in the space reserved for canned goods, and the canned goods where the soap should have gone.

Ethereal stopped sobbing and looked up. "Look what you're doing, Harry Hanson! You're just like your father! But I can tell you that I'm going to change all that. You're going to Boston. You're going to a proper school where the teacher doesn't take a week off to go deer hunting in fall and another week in spring when the walleyes are running.

"You're going to have a teacher who doesn't come to school with blood on his shirt and stinking like a fish. A school where children talk about other things than trapping and hunting helpless animals, and a school where the boys don't brag about whose father can get the biggest wad of chewing tobacco in his cheek!"

Hurry Up was completely unstrung now. He had never seen his mother carry on like this before. He dared a sidelong glance at her. There were tears on her cheeks and her upper lip was beaded with sweat. Her hair was stringy and uncombed. There was a smudge of dirt on her nose and one cheek.

He had never seen her other than well-groomed. She made a fetish of twice daily brushing her hair, always changing her dress before supper, never lounging around in pants the way other women did. He had never seen her without shoes, and now her shoes were kicked off and she was sitting barefoot.

How he managed to put the groceries away, he never knew, but at last they were all in place, and once more he started sidling toward the door.

"You stay right here, Harry Hanson Junior. You aren't going out so you can try to kill that fish. You think I don't know what you've been up to. You even think like a little savage!"

Hurry Up didn't know how thinking like a little savage was supposed to be. He did know that he was sorry for his mother, and that he was frightened, too. And he did know that he didn't want to go to Boston, because he didn't want to leave his father. What's more he liked it in the forest, because how in Boston could he go walking along Bittersweet Creek to come to Hemlock Cave or dunk his head in a spring of icy water?

He wondered too how she knew so much about the

muskie. Had she heard him go out in the night? Did she know the flashlight was missing?

"The end of the world!" Ethereal went on. "That's what this place is. The end of the world! In summer the temperature goes up over ninety degrees. In winter it goes down to forty below. In summer the leaves turn brown and the grass dries up and blows away. In winter the snow drifts so high even the plows can't clear the road, and a man has to make a trip on snowshoes just to get groceries."

Hurry Up hadn't thought about it that way before. Deep snow meant no school. Fun popping corn. Hot weather meant swimming, walking along the creek, dunking his head into the spring.

Ethereal dashed the tears from her eyes with an angry toss of her head. "If it isn't mosquitoes, it's wood ticks. If it isn't wood ticks, it's black flies. There's either too much rain or not enough. Do you know, Harry Hanson Junior, that ever since your father brought me to this Godforsaken place nearly eleven years ago, I've had to fight to grow even enough flowers for one bouquet. Nothing will grow in this rocky, sandy soil. It's good for nothing. Not even radishes!"

Hurry Up wanted to tell her that there were lots of flowers in the forest. But then, his mother never walked there. She said she was afraid of the deep forest.

"Who would live, when there's a whole United States full of civilized cities," Ethereal went on, "where you

have to be afraid a bear might break down the front
door or a wolf kill a pet cat?"

Well, Hurry Up had never heard of a bear breaking
down a front door or of any wolves eating anyone's pet
cat. Of course, there were wolves in the woods, but they
stayed away from people, and you did have to be careful
during blueberry picking time not to get between an old
she bear and her cubs.

Ethereal's head was back down on her arms and she
was crying softly again. "That's what I get for thinking a
little Midwest environment would broaden my perspec-
tive. That's what I get for coming to the University of
Wisconsin, and meeting and falling in love with a guy everybody calls Step-an'-a-half."

That was the first time Hurry Up had ever heard Ethereal call her husband by his nickname. He had often
heard others use the name, but never in his mother's
presence. Then it had always been Harry or Mr. Hanson.

"Step-an'-a-half," she repeated the name, and then
threw back her head. A wild sort of laughter came
through her tears.

Now Hurry Up was really frightened. He wondered
whether to duck out and let his mother get over it, or
whether to come close, put a hand on her arm, and try
to console her.

The sobs were louder now. Estelle, perhaps sensing
what was going on, began to whimper, even though her
stomach was full of warm milk and her diapers dry.

124

Then the baby threw the bottle out of the crib, and it went crashing to the floor and broke.

"Well, it isn't always going to be like this," Ethereal said, lifting her head and blowing her nose into the hem of her apron.

Now Hurry Up had seen everything. His mother, Ethereal Hanson, blowing her nose in the hem of her apron.

"It isn't always going to be like this," Ethereal repeated, "because as soon as the danger passes we're getting out of here. We're going east where people are civilized. Where people don't go around calling other people Goose Gait, Fish Fins, Ham Hocks, Sugar Plum . . . where there's some sanity, and where people use their God given names!"

Now Estelle began wailing, but Ethereal made no move to pick her up. Hurry Up stood frozen by the sink. He didn't know whether to pick the baby up, try to comfort his mother, or just duck out and head for the creek. Then Estelle and Ethereal were wailing, and finally Hurry Up broke down and started crying too.

TEN

At the sight of so much grief, Hurry Up wiped the tears from his eyes and fled out onto the porch. His mother's wailing quieted to sobs, but the baby continued to scream. Then, not knowing what to do or where to go, he headed up Bittersweet Creek in the direction of Hemlock Cave.

But today even being in the cave was no good. He went to the spring and washed his tear-stained face. Then he headed back toward the house. He couldn't leave his mother alone at a time like this. He had the uneasy feeling that it was his place to stay with Ethereal when she was so distraught, that it wasn't right for him to go off alone and leave her with the wailing baby.

He went quietly through the door expecting to find a disheveled woman, but to his great surprise, his mother had washed her face, combed her hair, and even changed into a fresh dress. Even the baby was quietly contemplating a rag doll which had become her security symbol.

Hurry Up couldn't understand how one minute his mother could be on the edge of hysteria, and the next seem so composed and fresh looking. There was even a half-smile on her face, just as though fires weren't threatening her home, and the north woods wasn't a prison keeping her from her beloved Boston.

Perhaps it was the secret of being an adult. He knew he couldn't do it—change faces that swiftly. But whatever it was, it gave Hurry Up a corresponding lift, and before lunch was over they were both laughing and talking as they once had during the days before the air had turned coppery, during the days before the leaves had shriveled, and the grass was still green, and the whole world was bright, shiny and beautiful.

Hurry Up went back outside with the good feeling, and it lasted until the sun once more had perspiration streaking his cheeks and wetting his overalls.

With his back against a birch, he sat where he could see the pier and let his mind find the old rut of revenge. As he sat the resentment against the muskie grew within him until, once again, he was thinking of ways to bring Spade Face to justice—to kill him. His mind traveled over all the legal methods of catching the fish with an artificial lure or live bait. He thought about spearing procedures, but decided the water was too deep at the point where the fish lay to get a spear through its scales.

Perhaps dynamite. Indians on the reservation regularly dynamited fish. It was a sure way, a positive way of killing every living thing within the area of the explosion.

Once he began contemplating the use of dynamite to destroy Spade Face, he couldn't help but feel that he had been thinking of it in the secret corners of his mind all the time. That it was no new thing, but that some part of his mind had been playing with the idea and only waiting to have it brought to the surface where it could be examined more thoroughly.

There would be repercussions. He could not keep such a thing as dynamite a secret. He would be punished severely. There was danger. Fashioning a bomb was not child's play, though he had seen his father blast enough stumps to know how to use the explosive.

It remained for him only to find the courage to go ahead with it, and then work out some of the minor details such as placing the bomb where it would be certain to kill the fish and remembering to put a long enough fuse to the dynamite so he could get out of the way before the blast occurred.

He looked to the house. All seemed quiet. He looked back down toward the pier. Not a wave wrinkled the coppery water. He looked up into the branches of the white birch. A robin sat there, its beak wide, feathers askew, panting in the heat.

There was dynamite in the shed in a rock-lined hole where the summer heat couldn't affect it. There was a trap door over the cache, a trap door with a ring on it for lifting. All he had to do was take the cover off the hole, bring up the box, and there packed in sawdust would be the lethal sticks—enough perhaps to blow a whole island right out of the lake.

Half a stick would be enough, but if he did it he would use a whole stick to make positive the fish didn't escape. A whole stick placed in a can packed with sand and a cap all set with a long fuse running right out to where he could light it and set off the blast.

Matches were all that he lacked. But he could manage that. There was a big box of blue and red tipped matches right on a small table next to the kerosene stove. He could get a handful without any trouble, and after that it wouldn't be long and that muskie would be blown to kingdom come.

He looked up at the house again. There wasn't a sound, or any sign of movement. Getting slowly to his feet he went across the lawn and up onto the porch. Again he listened. There was nothing.

He crossed the porch and peered through the screen door. He could hear his mother breathing slowly, rythmically. It sounded as though she might be asleep. He slowly opened the door and went in.

Ethereal was on the couch with the baby beside her. She was so beautiful in her sleep that Hurry Up felt a catch in his throat just looking at her. Her blonde hair was just touseled enough to make a halo around her white face. The baby's hair was wet with perspiration, and it curled around her forehead and fell in ringlets around her neck.

Hurry Up tiptoed in his bare feet across the room to the kerosene stove. His hand went out and his fingers curled around a handful of matches.

"Harry? That you?"

He froze. When he didn't answer, his mother queried again: "Harry?"

"Yes, Mother," he said.

"Did you want something?"

He turned slowly. She hadn't opened her eyes. "Just a drink," he lied.

"Well, be quiet. Don't wake the baby."

"Okay," he said softly. Then there was only the rhythmical breathing once again—a mother's breathing and the whisper of a small child's breath.

Harry's fingers closed over the matches. He didn't dare put them into his sweat-soaked overall pocket. So he held them in his hand. Then he turned and slowly tiptoed back across the room, opened the squeaky screen door just far enough to squeeze through, and was back out on the porch.

Only then could he breathe naturally, and he gulped air as though he'd been underwater for a long time and needed great quantities of oxygen.

When he was breathing more quietly, he went down the steps and back to the shed. Inside, he hid the matches on a two-by-four in back of a big monkey wrench. Then he went over to where the trap door, with its iron ring, hid the dynamite cache.

He was about to open it when he decided to check outside once more. So he went to the door to look out. There was only a red squirrel. It sat on an old rotting stump, eyes only half-open, blinking slowly as though it couldn't believe the world could become so hot, so dry, so smoky.

He went back in and kneeling in the dirt took hold of the iron ring. He lifted, but the door did not budge. It hadn't been opened in a long time. He tugged, and, finally getting to one knee, threw his weight into the effort. The door came up with a shower of dust.

He sneezed, let the door fall back, and then listened. For a moment there was nothing, but then a heat bug began shrilling somewhere back in the woods. He wished it would stop. The noise it made covered all other sounds. His mother might approach and he'd never hear her.

But she was sleeping, he told himself, and what would she come to the shed for anyway?

He lifted the door and slid it off to one side. There was the box, a heavy wooden box in the tiny, stone-lined cellar, and on top of the box was plainly marked: DYNAMITE.

He sat looking at it for a while, and then with a thumb and a forefinger tried the nuts which were

131

screwed down over washers to hold the cover in place. They turned easily. He took one off and pried the washer up with his finger. Then he removed the other nut and washer. He carefully placed them to one side, and then with both hands pried the cover off. At once there was the smell of sawdust, fresh because it was cooler in the hole, pungent because there was even a little moisture in the box.

He groped in the sawdust carefully, felt a stick of dynamite, closed his fingers over it, and then brought it out. He brushed away sawdust which clung to it, and then held it at arm's length. It looked harmless enough —like a short, round, wooden stick—and anyone not knowing would never guess it was capable of destruction, of death.

Carefully he lay the stick of dynamite to one side. Then he smoothed the sawdust in the box, put the cover back on and replaced the washers and nuts. After the cover was screwed down tightly, he put the trap door back in place. Then with both hands he sifted dust back over it so any who might come would never guess that the door had been recently opened.

Then he crept to the door for a look around. Heat waves shimmered upward from the sandy lawn to make the trees behind them dance and waver in the still air. But there was no sound from the house. The only sound came from the cicada, the heat bug—perhaps the only creature in all the wide world of this north country to be delighted by the weather. The sounds of its rejoicing were as sharp as the sounds a nail makes when it is drawn from a piece of wood with which it has lived for a long time.

Hurry Up went back to the dynamite. He looked about for a place to hide it. Then he took out a damp, red handkerchief, wrapped it up, and placed it carefully in back of a cluster of tools which stood in one corner.

The job done, he got up and walked outside as casually as if he'd only been looking for a hammer. He circled the house to see if there were any signs of activity, and then headed for the forest edge where the discarded cans were kept until there was time to take a load to the township dump.

The small heap of cans glistened and glinted in the sun, and he moved them about with a stick, looking for one long enough to contain his stick of dynamite. He finally found one.

The green label was still on the can, and in black letters the word "SAUERKRAUT" was written. It seemed inappropriate, so Hurry Up tore the label off. He could still smell the sharp odor of the sauerkraut, and there was even some mildew at the bottom of the can where a few drops of juice had not yet evaporated.

The cover was still attached, and that was important. It was bent back, and he tested if it would come forward to cover the can. It worked admirably. Then, while he was on the way back to the shack, it occurred to him that he had forgotten to get a blasting cap. He tried to remember where his father kept them, because it wasn't likely they'd be in the same hole with the dynamite.

The caps would probably be in the metal tackle box which his father used to keep a variety of tiny nuts, bolts, and screws.

He found the box on the bench and opened it. He took out the top tray, and there in the bottom wrapped in heavy wax paper were caps. He opened the brown envelope carefully, put his fingers in and brought out a blasting cap. He put the cap carefully on the two-by-four next to the matches. Then he rummaged through the bottom of the tool box until he found a roll of black tape.

Well, he was almost ready. There was a long coil of fuse in the wall cabinet, and he took a pliers from the bench and cut a twenty foot length. It was long enough. He had seen his father blow stumps with much less.

Now to make the bomb. Setting the cap was the problem. He didn't quite know how to do it. But he reasoned that if he taped the fuse and the cap together right alongside the stick of dynamite it would surely detonate.

Now for the first time he felt nervous. He went to the shed door and looked out. Not satisfied, he stepped outside. The cicada had stopped shrilling. He listened. There was nothing. He still wasn't satisfied. He walked around the house and came quietly up onto the porch. He listened again. He could hear Estelle cooing, but he could hear no sound made by his mother.

He went to the door and pressed his nose against the screen. He could see the baby. She was wide-eyed and, having crept from her mother's arms, was playing on the floor. Still Ethereal slept soundly, and now Hurry Up could see the toll the last four months had taken.

There were dark circles beneath her eyes. Her skin, instead of being fresh and flowery as when she washed it, was grayish. Her hair, although only recently combed, now strung out from her head and it was dry, lifeless as the dead grass on the lawn.

He turned away quickly and trotted through the hot sand around the house into the dim interior of the shed.

Quickly then, he got back to the business of building the bomb. He put the blasting cap to the side of the dynamite and holding the fuse over the top taped fuse to cap to dynamite stick. He taped the fuse almost the entire length of the stick before he was satisfied, and then, tearing the tape with his teeth, he put the stick of dynamite in the can.

The earth in the shed was hard packed, so he took the bomb outside to where the rain had once long ago washed up a rill of sand. He gathered handfuls of sand and filled the can. Then he pressed the lid of the can down, leaving only an opening large enough for the fuse, and his bomb was ready.

Except, how would he hang it on the pier? He didn't dare drop it into the water. That might scare the muskie off, out of range of the blast. He had to hang it from the pier, suspend it in the water just above Spade Face's lair.

He went back into the shed to look around. He was just about convinced that he could fashion a container from old wire, when a heap of gunny sacks in the corner caught his eye.

That was it! Hang the bomb over the side in a gunny sack. Drive a nail into the piling, put the bomb into the sack with the fuse trailing, and then hang it over the side.

He went over and, sorting sacks, picked one without holes. He put the bomb into it, tied the mouth of the bag into a knot, and then laid it down on the earthen floor.

It looked harmless enough—a lumpy, brown sack with a length of white fuse trailing like a snake from it. But he knew it was powerful enough to blow his own home right off its foundation.

He picked up the bomb again and hid it in the corner where the gunny sacks lay. Then he got a nail and hammer and went to the pier. Quietly as was possible, he drove the nail a little way into the piling alongside which the muskie lay. Several times while tapping the nail into the wood, he looked up toward the house to see if his mother had decided to investigate the noise, but there was no sign of her.

When the nail was solidly implanted in the piling, he got up and went up to the house. He quietly crossed the porch and looked in through the screen. His mother was still sleeping. Estelle had crept over to the screen door, and when she saw him she made excited noises. He quickly ducked out of sight.

When he was down off the porch he trotted around the cottage. Now he couldn't wait. He didn't dare wait. If he waited now he'd lose his nerve. He knew he had to do it now or he would never do it. In his mind he could see splinters of the pier flying through the air. The water would somewhat muffle the explosion, but there would be a roar loud enough to bring Ethereal hurrying from the house to see what had happened. Well, it was the price, and he was prepared to pay it.

He put the hammer back into the tool box, went to the two-by-four and took down the matches. Then pushing aside the gunny sacks, he brought out the bomb.

He went to the door and stood there for several minutes listening. The cicada had started shrilling again, and the noise made him nervous.

Perhaps he'd better wait. Maybe sometime when his mother was gone. But she never left during these days of danger, except to make a quick trip to Twin Forks for ice and groceries.

No, he had to do it now or he knew he never would. If he stopped to think about the repercussions, if he stopped to consider what his parents might have in store for him, he knew he would never light the fuse. It had to be now, or he had to disassemble the bomb, put the cap and dynamite back, and hang the length of fuse in the cabinet.

He made himself think about the muskie lying down there in the comparatively cool water, in the shade, at peace only because there was no one to challenge him. He thought about his fox, saw again the tiny intestines floating on the water.

He'd do it! He'd end that fish forever! Now or never, he told himself.

He started from the shed and the cicada ceased shrilling. The silence was so profound that he stopped in his tracks. It was as though the heat had killed every woodland thing. Usually, on such a cloudless day, there should have been bird song and squirrel chatter. There should have been cricket sounds and the whine of mosquitoes. There should have been the sound of waves on the shore, against the pier, and the snarl of a fisherman's motor out on the lake. There should have been the whirl of terns over the water, the war whoop of the kingfisher, the cry of a loon. But, instead, there was only deathly silence, a quiet which seemed to bore right into the boy, get through his skin until it had become a part of the bone.

Hurry Up shook himself. He couldn't afford to be mesmerized by the stillness. Not now. He had come too far to let even this unearthly quiet stop him. He circled the house, trying to hold the gunny sack against the far side of his body so that even if his mother was watching, she wouldn't see it.

His eyes were on the house as he walked, but there

was no sign of activity. His bare feet touched the hot boards of the pier. He put the bomb down and leaned over to make certain the fish was in position. He wanted no explosion if the muskie was not there. This had to be it. He knew he'd never get another chance. After the bomb went off, the muskie had to be dead, because he would surely get no second chance. Once his parents knew he had exploded dynamite to kill the fish, they would put the bay off limits to him, and he'd probably even have to stay in the house for a week or a month.

He was sweating so much his eyes stung, and he had to wait a long time before he was able to see Spade Face. But the muskie was there, right alongside the piling. The dynamite would drive his body right into the bottom of the lake.

Hurry Up got back up. Now he worked swiftly. There was no turning back. He lowered the gunny sack gently into the water. He hung the knotted sack on the nail so that the can with the stick of dynamite was just below the surface. Then he trailed the fuse along the boards of the pier in the direction of the shore.

He couldn't stop now—not for anything. He laid the matches down beside the end of the fuse. Then he picked one up with his brown fingers and, holding it hard, struck it along the boards. It broke. He picked up another and scratched it over a nail head showing through the pier. It sputtered, flared briefly, and went out.

His fingers trembled. He had to control himself. What

was the matter with these matches. Had his sweating hands so dampened them they wouldn't light? But he had been so careful.

He took another, scratched it over the nail head, watched it flare. After the first brief explosion of flame, he could hardly see the fire in the heat of the day.

Carefully he lifted the end of the fuse and held it to the flame. It sputtered, went out, sputtered again and went out again, and then the match went out.

Now he began to shake all over. He took a deep breath to control the shaking. Then he quickly scratched another match over the nail head and, when it was burning, held it to the fuse.

This time the fuse caught. He could hear it sizzle as well as see the tiny sparks cascade around it. He could smell it too, and there was a very faint trail of smoke.

He waited another three seconds to make sure the fuse was burning, and then got to his feet and ran. At the end of the pier he turned toward Bittersweet Creek. His heels dug in and sent the sand flying. Then, where flood waters had eroded the earth from around a huge rock, he found his shelter.

Throwing himself to the ground, he lay panting for a few moments. He turned on his stomach and got to his knees. Carefully he lifted his head to peer over the top of the rock. He could see the fuse. It was burning swiftly. In less than a half-minute Spade Face would be blasted to kingdom come.

140

Hurry Up had almost expected to feel some great surge of joy because at last the muskie's death warrant was signed, but all he felt was tired. Lying there against the hot rock, he could understand what his mother meant when at the end of a hard day she sometimes said: "I feel limp as a washed-out dishrag."

Well, he felt washed-out, too. He was done in. He was exhausted. He was too overcome to feel triumphant.

There was nothing now, nothing except to wait for the explosion, see Spade Face's demolished body, and then take his punishment.

He started to close his eyes briefly against the heat, but a movement along the path from the house to the pier caused him to widen his eyes in disbelief and horror.

It couldn't be! Not now! Of all times!

Crawling down the sandy path was his baby sister, Estelle. She must have pushed the screen door open and crawled off the porch.

"No! No! Go back!" Hurry Up meant to scream the words, but they came out in a whisper.

He was about to race out from behind the rock to grab up the baby and make a run for the house when the screen door slammed and Ethereal came bounding from the house.

"Estelle! Estelle!" she was screaming. Fear of water had always been with her. Now she thought it was threatening her baby.

Hurry Up watched his mother run along the path,

bend over and pick up the baby. He thought: She has been saved. They'll go back to the house. Everything will be all right. Ethereal will take Estelle out of harm's way.

But instead of walking back toward the house, Ethereal continued on down the path toward the water, on down the path toward the pier, on down the path to where the fire was eating swiftly the dwindling length of fuse so the flame could crawl down inside the gunny sack, detonate the bomb and cause the explosion.

ELEVEN

In the days and weeks and months to come, Hurry Up often tried to remember exactly what had happened next, but somehow he wasn't able. Perhaps it was because his mind refused to admit that it might have been responsible for such a tragic occurrence.

Hurry Up often wondered about it, because he had been led to believe that when an especially tragic event was about to occur, the mind caught up every last detail of the action preceding it. Then it would be imprinted on the brain so there was never any forgetting.

In the books he had been able to read, Hurry Up remembered how the hero could remember even the color of the rocks he passed while falling into a canyon, or how a fly had crawled across the gun barrel at the precise moment when the hero fired the shot to save the heroine's life.

143

Well, no such thing had happened to Hurry Up. He never knew that the cicada had started shrilling again. He never knew that he had jumped to his feet and shouted: "Go back! Go back! Dynamite!" And that his mother had only stood there at the edge of the pier looking at him as if she didn't know what he was talking about.

He never even remembered the terror which ripped the breath right out of his lungs and squeezed his stomach into a tight knot. He never remembered waving his hands, or the tears which shot up to pour from his eyes, but then suddenly dried without being spilled.

He couldn't remember that he started out from around the rock, but then stubbed his feet on a projection and fell flat in the hot sand, and that the sand was in his eyes and his nose and his mouth.

Try as he would in the days after, he couldn't remember jumping to his feet and running along the sandy beach. It was as though the camera of his mind had ceased for a time to take pictures, so there was nothing except a blank.

People told him that he had almost knocked his mother over in his haste to get around her and onto the pier. And he had to believe them, because he had no evidence to either contradict or affirm his actions.

Try as he might, he couldn't remember racing along the hot boards, reaching down for the sack containing

144

the bomb, and then with a mighty heave giving it an arcing toss that landed it far out in the bay.

He couldn't remember any of that, but he could remember from that point on. He could remember the gunny sack with the bomb hitting the water, sinking a little way; and the geyser of water shooting almost as high as the trees as the dynamite exploded.

He sank down then to the pier and the tears flowed. His mother turned and ran with the baby back to the house. After Estelle was safely in the crib, she came back down and, taking an arm, lifted him to his feet. Then with one arm around his shoulders, she led him back to the house.

The tears stopped when he got to the kitchen table and sank back into a chair. His mother went to the ice box and brought out the lemonade pitcher and poured two glasses. Then they sat for a long, long time without saying anything.

Finally his mother broke the silence. "Harry, why did you do it?"

He looked down at his scarred toes. To say that he had made a dynamite bomb merely to kill a fish suddenly seemed insane, so he said nothing.

"Look at me, Harry," his mother said. "Look at me, and tell me whatever got into you."

But he couldn't look up. Try as he might, he could not lift his eyes to look into his mother's.

"We could have been killed," his mother said.

A shiver ran through Harry despite the fact that his body was wet with sweat and the heat in the cottage was almost stifling.

"Drink some of your lemonade," Ethereal said.

Hurry Up put the glass to his lips, but he couldn't swallow and let the liquid run from his mouth back into the glass.

"It's this awful country," Ethereal said. "It's this barbaric land!"

Hurry Up squeezed his eyes shut as though he could erase everything that had happened and make the world right again.

"You know you should be punished," Ethereal finally said.

At that Hurry Up nodded.

"But who's going to do it? You might as well have no father at all. Out of the last one hundred days he hasn't been home more than four. This is a terrible land. This is a place for savages. No civilized people should live here."

Hurry Up lifted his eyes just enough to take a peek at his mother's face. The lines of fatigue and sadness were turning into lines of anger. He looked back down at his toes, at the scrubbed white kitchen floor.

"Well, if for all practical purposes you don't have a father, then I suppose I've got to be both mother and father," Ethereal said. Her voice was rising. Hurry Up detected a hint of hysteria in it, but all he could manage was a nod.

"Where did you get the dynamite?" Ethereal asked. And then without waiting for an answer she said: "From the shed, I suppose. The stump dynamite. That's it. Isn't it?"

Again Hurry Up managed a small nod.

"How do you think you would help your dead fox by killing that fish?" his mother asked.

Hurry Up shook his head, slowly from side to side.

"It's incredible! If I told your grandparents they'd think I was inventing the story. They'd never believe it. Fact is, I can't even believe it myself though I just saw it happen."

Hurry Up felt tears starting up near the back of his eyes and he strove vainly to keep them from spilling over again.

Ethereal was talking. "Well, one thing is for sure. That ends it for us in this place. I've really had it now. We're going to Boston. If your father doesn't want to come along, he can stay here. I'll not live in a place where ten-year-old boys are brought up so wild they have to dynamite a fish to get their revenge."

Though he hadn't really meant to, Hurry Up nodded again.

"Meanwhile," Ethereal went on, "what are we going to do about you? Something like this can't go unpunished. You've got to learn that it's wrong to steal dynamite that isn't yours. You've got to realize it is a terrible thing to endanger your own life and the lives of those around you by causing such an explosion. But how do I make you see it?"

Hurry Up shrugged his shoulders as though to say he didn't know.

The shrug irritated Ethereal. Her voice lifted. "Well, I'll tell you what's to be done. You're going to get whipped so that you'll forever remember. If I can't make any progress by talking to you, I'll have to leave such an imprint on your bottom that every time you get a notion to do some crazy thing, you'll remember it and think twice."

Hurry Up dared to look up. His mother's usually white face had turned pink.

"And," Ethereal went on, "since your father isn't here to do it, it would seem that I have to. Do you hear me, Harry? Do you hear me? I'm going to whip you. I'm going to whip you even if you did save our lives. I'm going to whip you because it was you who put our lives in danger."

His mother had never whipped him. For that matter, neither had his father. A cuff behind the ears had been the extent of his corporal punishment. But somehow now he almost welcomed a whipping. Maybe it would wash away the terrible feeling which ate away at his insides.

"To think," Ethereal said, "that I have to take a stick and thrash my own boy. To think that I must do the

148

punishing because there's never a father around to do the job of disciplining his own son."

Hurry Up squirmed in his chair.

"Squirm," Ethereal said, "You should squirm. Supposing that dynamite had gone off while Estelle and I were standing there." Then, as if remembering sharply again, she got up and almost ran over to the crib where the baby had been playing with her toes. She jerked the baby from the crib, smothered it with a hug and then put her back down.

"I'm going to whip you, Harry Hanson Junior. I'm going to whip you, and then so long as you live you'll never forget this day."

Hurry Up knew that a whipping wasn't necessary to make him remember. How could he ever forget it?

"And you're going to cut a stick for me," his mother said. "You're going to take the butcher knife and go outside and cut me a stick and bring it back in here and then I'm going to whip you."

Hurry Up nodded that he would.

"Well, get up then. Go get that butcher knife, and cut me a birch switch. Go, Harry. Do it!"

Hurry Up looked bewildered. His mother's tone of voice was metallic, high-pitched.

"Do you hear me, Harry. Get that butcher knife. Now! Go get it! Go out there and cut me a switch!"

More than the words, it was the way Ethereal said it

that jerked Hurry Up out of his chair. He stood there, sweat streaking his cheeks where there were already tear stains, his short, straw-colored hair askew, his overalls dark with sweat.

"Do it, Harry! Get that knife! Cut a switch!" Ethereal's voice went up almost a whole octave until it was like the whine of a high-speed saw. Then, when Hurry Up didn't move, she reached out and, grabbing him by the front of his overalls, shouted: "Now, Harry! Now!"

Hurry Up half walked and half stumbled across the kitchen to the cabinet. "Get it, Harry. Get it!" He heard his mother's voice. He opened the drawer and took out the knife. Then he turned, and without looking at his mother crossed the kitchen and went out the door.

The heat was blinding as he walked across the sand to the birch clump with its shriveled leaves. He took hold of a small branch at the tip and hacked it from the trunk of the tree. He trimmed the tiny limbs from it quickly, and then started back toward the house.

It was only then that it really dawned on him that his mother meant to thrash him. It was an incredible thing to contemplate. Suddenly he wanted to turn away from the house, throw the switch and the knife down. He wanted to run up Bittersweet Creek and crawl in the Hemlock Cave and never come out again.

But his bare feet took him unerringly toward the kitchen door. Step by step across the lawn, up the two

150

steps, over the cracked boards of the porch. But at the screen door he stopped. He couldn't go in.

"Come in, Harry. Come in. I see you!"

He went in and put the knife and the stick down on the kitchen table.

"You call that a switch! You call that a stick!"

For the first time he really looked at the birch switch he had cut. It was a tiny stick. He could see there wasn't enough body to it to spank a kitten. But he had grabbed the first switch to come to hand.

"You call that a stick! You think you can get out of this whole unspeakable adventure by getting a few licks with that twig!" His mother sounded furious.

She brushed past him, swept up the kitchen knife from the table, and banged out through the screen door.

Hurry Up felt faint. He reached for the chair back to brace himself, and then eased himself down onto the chair.

Estelle had begun to cry. Ordinarily Hurry Up would have gone over to the crib to comfort her. But now he just sat there like a boy carved from stone. He didn't even blink his eyes, but only held himself taut, waiting for the screen door to announce with a bang that his mother was back.

He heard her come up the steps. He heard the screen door open, but he did not look around.

"Now, Harry, you listen. This punishment is going to

be yours because you've acted like an animal, and an animal can't understand some things unless you whip it." Ethereal's voice was so calm that Hurry Up had to look up in spite of himself, because he couldn't believe that once again she could be wearing another face.

The anger had gone out of her eyes. Her face was white again. Her lips were slightly apart and full and red and she was breathing naturally.

"Now you get up off that chair and you lie across it," Ethereal said.

Hurry Up couldn't believe he was hearing his mother. It would almost have been better if the bomb had gone off in his hands, because this wasn't going to be a punishment delivered in a moment of anger, but a deliberate whipping.

"Harry, did you hear me? Across that chair."

Still Hurry Up sat there.

"Harry Hanson Junior!" There was no mistaking her. She meant it.

He got up slowly, turned to her, opened his mouth as though to plead for mercy. Then he closed it.

"Across the chair, Harry."

Across the chair! But he couldn't. He was ten. In the north country a boy could be counted almost a man by the time he was ten, and in times of great danger boys of ten went out on the fire line to fight the fires. So to lay himself across a chair so his mother might beat him with a birch stick . . .

He felt her hand on his shoulder. Anger boiled up in him. He shrugged her hand off. Then he turned his back on her, faced the chair, and in a swift gesture of rage threw himself across the hard wooden seat.

"Now I want you to know why I'm doing this," his mother said, as he lay waiting for the first blow. "I want you to know that it is because you had enough hate in your heart for—of all things—a fish, to endanger the lives of your whole family. I want you to understand that at no time while you are a boy or a man do you let hate or anger or any emotion so rule your conduct that you endanger either yourself or any other person. When you let your emotions rule you, you are an animal—not a man or even a boy."

Ethereal stopped talking and walked around to where she could swing the stick. Estelle was howling now, and Ethereal had to shout to be heard.

"Do you understand me, Harry? Do you understand!"

She raised the stick high, holding it for a second as though to aim the blow. And then the telephone rang.

Three long rings!

The stick stopped moving in mid-air. There it was again.

Three long rings!

The signal to run, get out. The emergency call. The signal which meant the fires had finally broken through the cordon of men and machines and was running wild.

Three long rings!

TWELVE

The shrill ringing of the phone cut through the child's wailing like a fire siren through the darkest, most smoke-filled night. Three long rings. The birch stick clattered to the floor.

Harry felt the urgency of the situation. He jumped to his feet, looked around wildly, and then waited for his mother to speak.

Three more long rings!

Ethereal ran outside, leaving her shoes in the house. For a moment Hurry Up stayed behind to look at the wailing baby, and then he ran after her.

He wasn't two steps off the porch when he knew something was different. His mother's hair was waving out, blowing away from her head. There was a wind. It had arisen while they were in the house.

Ethereal was shading her eyes, looking over the tops

of the trees which surrounded the clearing. Already the tears had dried on her face. Now it was streaked only with dirt where she had tried to wipe away the dust. As she squinted at the sky he could see worry wrinkles on her forehead and crow's feet just above her cheek bones.

"Well, I can't see any smoke," she finally said, "so maybe it isn't too bad."

Meanwhile the telephone kept ringing—three long rings and then a pause, then three more long rings.

Then suddenly it was quiet, and as if on signal, the baby stopped squalling too. Still mother and son stood in the sand where tufts of dry, brown grass stood like the empty little tents of an ant army.

Suddenly his mother was galvanized into action. "Now, Harry, you listen," she said, calmly but with such strength that his head snapped about so he was facing her. "Now you listen," she repeated, "we've got to get our supplies into the truck, pick up Mrs. Canuck, and then head for Otter City."

"But I thought we were going to try to save the house," Hurry Up said.

"Not on three long rings. That means business. That means run. And now you run. Water jug in the front seat. Blankets and canvas and pails in the back with the food." She had started toward the house, and she talked as she ran: "And when we get to Mrs. Canuck's place you get in back, and Mrs. Canuck will sit up front with me to hold the baby. Now move!"

Hurry Up started toward the house, and then spun in his tracks when she said: "No! Wait!" He looked at her, waiting.

"I'll get the blankets, water and food," she said. "You go around to the shed and get an axe, two shovels and the saw. We might need them."

She rushed past him, and he turned to go around the house. He had to make two trips, and by then she had the emergency equipment from the house in the truck, and had gone back to get Estelle.

When she came out with the baby in her arms, she stood in the exact center of the clearing, scanning the sky above the tree line. Except for the thin white smoke which had been in the air for so many days Hurry Up couldn't remember the sky looking otherwise, there were no signs of fire.

But now the wind was shredding the mist of white smoke, tearing at it, so there were long steamers of white and an occasional slit through which he got glimpses of blue sky.

He stood there, feeling the wind in his hair, feeling it whip playfully around his overall legs, feeling it like a strange, cool hand on his hot, red face. His mother stood too, and her blonde hair was blowing back. Suddenly she didn't look like his mother, but like a picture he'd seen of a wood carving of a woman on the bow of a viking boat.

It seemed she would stand forever, head high, chin

tilted upward, hair streaming. Then Estelle whimpered and the spell was broken.

"Into the truck," she said, motioning to Hurry Up. And when he had jumped up to the high front seat, she handed the baby up and went around to the driver's seat.

She turned the key, stepped on the starter, and for a moment Hurry Up thought the engine wasn't going to catch. Suddenly it roared, and Ethereal eased up on the gas until the pistons were hammering with such reassurance that Hurry Up felt certain the old truck would get them out.

Still he wasn't afraid. Up to now he hadn't seen anything to be afraid of. He had been more frightened of his mother's mood. But now? What was there? They'd pick up Mrs. Shoot First, and then he'd get in back and they'd drive out to the main road and on down to Otter City.

Estelle stirred in his arms, and he couldn't resist planting his cracked, dry lips on her moist forehead where the blonde hair was falling in silken ringlets. The baby stirred at the touch and looked up at him. He held her closer.

When the truck didn't move, he looked over at his mother. She had put the stick shift back in neutral and was opening the door. "You sit still," she said, "and I'll be right back." She ran around the back of the truck and up the sandy path and disappeared into the house.

When she came back out she was holding something,

but Hurry Up couldn't see what it was until she was back behind the wheel and had put it up on the truck dash. It was the framed picture of her mother and father standing in front of a large house with white pillars. He hadn't thought about it before, but now he supposed it was the house she had lived in while a little girl in Boston.

He had never had the occasion to give much thought to his Boston grandparents, but, now that he could see them lying at an odd angle there before him, he guessed they'd be nice people to live with, but never nice enough to make up for all the things he'd have to leave—like Bloody Burn Bay and Turnabout Lake, with trees coming right down to the water and deer coming to drink any morning you were out early enough to see them.

Ethereal had the truck in reverse and it made a grinding sound as she backed it around. Hurry Up braced himself against the bumps and, still clutching the baby, spread his elbows for balance.

Then his mother put the truck in low and they began to move slowly down the sandy tire tracks, down the dim road almost hidden by the branches which closed over it. They went around the curves slowly in second gear, and Ethereal skillfully dodged a rock here, a limb in another place, and almost came to a complete stop when a deer came wildly catapulting straight for them, turning off only at the last possible moment to avoid being struck.

"The fire must be coming," Etheral said. "That deer was running blind!"

When they came to the gravel road, Ethereal stopped the truck and leaning forward looked both ways before easing out onto it. Then she turned north, and he could hear the stones kicking up under the fender as the truck picked up speed.

At a white mailbox on a white post, she slowed the truck and turned in onto a road which looked almost identical to theirs. He read the name on the mailbox: Sam Canuck, but it wouldn't have been necessary, because he knew where everyone lived.

The truck crawled slowly along the winding dirt road, and then the forest broke open and there was a clearing almost identical in size to the one in which their house stood. There was Bloody Burn Bay kicking up a good chop of waves, and the willows along the shore bending in the wind.

Mrs. Shoot First was standing out in the yard, a pillowcase filled with her belongings on the ground beside her. She was holding her huge stomach with both hands, but when she saw the truck she took a step forward and waved excitedly, just as though she had expected they might not come.

Ethereal put the truck in neutral and braked it to a halt. Then she climbed down and, with the engine still running, walked up to Mrs. Shoot First.

Once again it seemed to Hurry Up that he was seeing Mrs. Shoot First for the very first time. He had never thought to take a good look at her, but now that he did

159

he could see how pretty she was—dark as his mother was blonde, as full and heavy with the baby as his mother was slim and willowy.

There were tears on Mrs. Shoot First's face. Hurry Up could hear her voice, which had a shrill edge to it, even above the growl of the truck motor. "Oh, I don't know, Ethereal. I don't know. I don't know . . ." she kept repeating.

"It will be all right," he heard his mother reassure her. "Everything is going to be fine." She put an arm around Mrs. Shoot First's shoulders to give her a little hug.

She picked up the pillowcase of belongings and going around threw it into the rear of the truck. Then she came around to Hurry Up's side of the vehicle and indicated that he should hand the baby down. When he had, she said: "Now you help me get Mrs. Canuck into the truck, and then you crawl in back."

Mrs. Shoot First came around the truck slowly, still holding her stomach with both hands. She squared herself in front of the truck door and put up her arms, getting a grasp on the open window with one and a hold on the back door post with the other. She put a foot on the fender and started to pull herself up.

"Now you help," Ethereal said sharply to Hurry Up. Except that Hurry Up didn't know how to help except to brace his small hands on her rather wide beam and push. So he did just that, but looked down at the ground so he wouldn't have to know about how he was pushing her on

160

the butt, while she groaned and grunted. Finally he felt her lift away from him as she made it to the high front seat.

Mrs. Canuck made no motions to get herself comfortable, but only sat there with a pained expression on her face. "You all right?" Ethereal asked.

"Oh, I don't know. I don't know," the woman said.

"What do you mean, you don't know?" Ethereal asked, a little irritation in her voice.

"It's just that . . . well, I'm so uncomfortable, and maybe it's all because of this terrible heat."

Ethereal hesitated before handing Estelle up, as though she might be thinking of putting the baby into the back of the truck. Then she said: "Here, you'll have to hold Estelle. Can you do it?"

"The baby? Of course. Of course, I can hold the baby." She reached out with both arms, and Ethereal gave her Estelle.

"Into the back with you," Ethereal said, turning to Hurry Up who stood watching.

Hurry Up grabbed the sides of the truck, put his bare feet to a tire, and pulled himself up. Then he vaulted over and onto the blankets.

Before getting back into the truck Ethereal again scanned the sky above the fringe of trees, but there were no signs up there that the fire was coming.

They drove slowly down the winding road, but once out on the gravel, Ethereal pressed down on the gas. The stones beat a steady staccato on the undersides of the fenders, and some went shooting back down the road and some off into the roadside ditches with its wilted weeds.

Hurry Up was enjoying the ride. He had forgotten about the fire, about Mrs. Canuck and her big stomach, about Ethereal's determination to leave the north woods. All that mattered now was that the truck was whizzing along at such a rate that the trees in passing were blurred, that the wind was so strong on his face it brought tears to his eyes.

Blankets flapped all around him, and even the edge of the heavy canvas lifted, so he gathered them all together and brought them closer to the cab of the truck where they'd be out of the slipstream. Then he got to his feet and, hanging to the cab to keep from being bounced out, looked straight ahead into the rushing wind.

Perhaps he saw the deer even before Ethereal. Four of them were coming in great bounds heading through the trees straight for the road. Hurry Up even shouted: "Look out! Look out!" But, of course, Ethereal couldn't hear him.

Then a panic-stricken doe crashed into the side of the truck right above a rear tire, and the vehicle went skidding sideways. The bumper lightly struck another deer, and the truck turned completely around and in a cloud of dust and a rattle of stones came to a stop.

The abrupt stop threw Hurry Up to the truck bed, and

for a moment he was stunned. Then he got to his knees and looked over the side. The doe was lying on the road. From the angle of its head, he knew the neck was broken. Ethereal was out in the road beside the doe. He heard her voice: "You all right? Hurry Up, you all right?"

For a moment the boy forgot the fire. She had called him Hurry Up! For the first time she had used his nickname.

Finally he said: "I'm all right, Ethereal."

"Is the deer dead?" she asked.

"The deer is dead."

"Look now, Harry" (this time it was Harry again), "be careful because we're in trouble." She was pointing down the road. A couple of miles ahead he could see billows of white smoke rising above the trees. All at once, and for the first time, he was frightened.

"Now you listen, Harry," she went on, "we've got to try to get through. I'm going to roll up the windows, and if there is fire cover yourself with the canvas. You hear, Harry!" She had started shouting, but now she resumed a normal tone. "Poor deer," she said, starting back toward the cab of the truck.

The motor started willingly, and Ethereal eased the truck around so it was pointed toward the spear of fire. Then, just as the vehicle was starting forward, Hurry Up saw a fawn step out of a waist-high stand of brown bracken and proceed haltingly toward the dead doe.

The boy was on his feet in an instant. His first instinct was to leap over the side of the truck, but already it was going too fast. So he scrambled along the truck bed and began beating on the rear window of the cab.

"Stop! Stop!" he shouted.

Slowly the truck came to a halt and instantly Hurry Up was over the side. Without waiting to tell his mother why he had shouted for her to stop, he ran back down the road. The fawn was nuzzling its mother. In spite of the heat it was shivering. The boy approached it slowly, and then when it didn't run he swept it up in his arms.

The fawn struggled only briefly and then lay quietly in Hurry Up's arms, and he walked back to the truck. His mother was out in the roadbed.

"It can't be more than a month old," Hurry Up said, and then, by way of explanation: "It'll die if we leave it."

Ethereal only nodded, but when Hurry Up couldn't get the animal up over the high sides, she took it from him and gently laid it on the canvas. The boy thanked her with his eyes and scrambled aboard.

Ethereal got back into the cab. The truck gears meshed with a clatter. Slowly they began moving.

The fawn lay flat, its ears back. Hurry Up pulled a blanket over it and then sprinkled water on its head.

Sometimes now Hurry Up got a glimpse of flames leaping above the treetops. Billows of white smoke shrouded even the nearest trees. Sometimes sparks show-

164

ered over the truck, and the roar of the fire was louder than that of the old truck engine.

Hurry Up sprinkled himself and the fawn with water again. Then he kneeled so he could look around the cab at the road ahead. At intervals deer leaped across. There were smaller animals too—two brush wolves, a fox, three otters humping along in single file, numerous red squirrels—all running panic-stricken out ahead of the flames.

Now the heat of the fire pressed around them. Hurry Up wondered how they could ever get through. Flames had closed in. He could see them leaping from the crown of one tree to the crown of the next.

Getting off his knees he lay down next to the fawn and pulled the blanket over himself. What was his mother thinking! They'd never get through. They'd be burned to a crisp if they drove further into that field of fire.

Abruptly the truck stopped. He heard his mother's voice. She had rolled down a window and was leaning out. "Hurry Up, we've got to go back. We can't get through! I'll have to try the other road. Cover up!"

Then she rolled the window up and he lay down again on his side, pressing close to the fawn. He could feel how she had to wrestle the wheel. Six times she had to go backward and then forward before she got the truck turned around on the narrow gravel road.

Once straightened out they were running from the fire,

and for the first quarter-mile it seemed his mother drove at top speed, thinking, perhaps, only to flee and risk the chance of hitting any deer which might be passing.

Then there was no heat, and the wind felt good on his face again, and the sound of the gravel under the fenders was a comforting sound of their progress.

It was the long way around to Otter City, but surely now, the only way out. Maybe twenty miles, Hurry Up thought, whereas it was only twelve if they had taken the short cut through the fire.

Well, the boy thought, as he watched the trunks of white birch and darker pines flash by, if nothing else they could always go back home and put out in a boat and sit on the lake while the fire swept by. They might douse themselves with buckets of water to stay cool or extinguish any burning brands or sparks carried to them on the wind.

But retreat to the lake didn't seem likely. They were cruising along and there were no signs of fire. The gas tank was full. The engine roared with confidence. The stones were a soothing rattle against the undersides of the fenders. The wind kept caressing both him and the fawn. He could see his mother through the window, her head bent over the wheel, and when he raised himself, he saw muscles in her bare forearms that he had never suspected were there.

Past their road. Past Canuck's mailbox. Past Twin Corners. Past Goose Gait's road. Past the widow's road.

His mother drove the truck as if she were fiercely determined not to be stopped, and Hurry Up felt pride at her performance.

She was strong! She was capable! She *could* fight! And he was surprised that he had never noticed it before.

He took the cap from a water jug and, pouring a little into a cupped palm, held it for the deer. When the fawn would not drink he wetted the soft muzzle, and the tiny deer reached for the moisture with a curling, pink tongue.

Five miles, ten . . . and then it struck Hurry Up like lightning can come to a tree: There was smoke up ahead! He got to his knees to make sure. There was no mistaking it. Smoke billowed across the road less than a mile ahead.

Still the truck kept moving at a steady pace. Tongues of flame showed themselves leaping wildly to lash at the tops of the conifers. Then the truck came to a gravel sliding halt.

His mother got down and came back. "Hurry Up, we're trapped!" For a full ten seconds neither mother nor son said anything as they looked into each other's eyes as though they might read some way out of their predicament. Then it was Hurry Up who spoke: "The lake. It's the only way. We've got to go back, take the boat and some buckets and get out on the lake!"

THIRTEEN

Ethereal turned the truck around, but this time she did not speed, but only fed the vehicle enough gas so it moved steadily away from the fire, back past the little roads which marked the shore homes of their friends, until they came to their own drive. The truck went slowly off the gravel onto the sandy trail which was their drive. But then, when they were in their clearing, she did not kill the motor, but turned the truck around so it was facing in the direction from which they'd come.

Hurry Up waited. Ethereal got down and came around. "Hurry Up," she said in a strained and almost inaudible voice, "Mrs. Canuck is getting ready to have her baby today."

The statement did not startle the boy. It held no real meaning for him. He jumped down beside her and looking up asked: "Can she have it in the boat?"

Ethereal shook her head. "She can't have it anywhere here. I know how terrible that can be. You know I was alone. Somehow we've got to get her out of here."

It was too much for Hurry Up to assimilate, so he reached for the water jug and, tilting it, drank.

Hurry Up wanted to ask some questions, but a moan from Mrs. Shoot First cut him short.

"Oh my Lord, my Lord, my Lord," Ethereal said, and Hurry Up saw tears start up in her eyes. She brushed a hand fiercely across her face. "Get in," she commanded. "We're going through!"

The fawn's head was up when Hurry Up clambered back into the truck. He touched the spotted creature, saw his own image in the large liquid eyes, and then the truck started to move.

Ethereal drove at a moderate pace. Hurry Up pulled back the blanket and wetted the fawn down. Then he poured water over himself. At the turn-out Ethereal turned left. She was going to run the fire gantlet along the short route.

The boy lay down, squirming halfway around to watch for the fire. Once he got a glimpse of a deer which came perilously close. Another time there was a soft thud as the front tires apparently hit something, and then a sharp thump as the rear wheels went over it.

The fawn had closed its eyes now, but Hurry Up was sure it wasn't sleeping. He wet a rag and sponged the animal's muzzle and then its entire head.

169

The truck was losing momentum. He could feel it. He got to his knees to look out ahead. Then the truck stopped, and Ethereal was out and back beside him.

"Everything all right?" she asked.

Hurry Up nodded.

"That's good. Now keep covered because we're going through. Keep one eye out and open. If a blanket or anything catches fire, put it out."

Hurry Up got to his feet. He had to see what they were getting into. Then he saw. On each side were skeleton pines, their branches black, and smoke curling up their trunks to be caught and run out in streamers on the wind. The roadway itself was littered with smoldering branches, burning embers, and even while he watched a tall pine started slowly earthward. It fascinated him to see how slowly it fell, and then how it picked up speed and at last crashed in a shower of ashes, smoke and embers.

At last he spoke: "You mean you're going through that?"

"We have to. We have to go through, Hurry Up."

He looked at her and, young as he was, he thought it was the first time he had really seen her. She was strong. He could feel it.

"Let's go," he said, sinking back to his knees.

The truck started slowly forward. The fawn lifted its head and then put it down again. Hurry Up pulled the blanket up to his chin. Then they pierced the wall of white smoke. It was suffocating and the boy coughed. The fawn lunged forward and Hurry Up had to hold it down.

He wondered how his mother could see to drive. He could barely make out the fringe of forest along the road. He could feel the tires going over branches. Bright lights winked off and on as the fire found resin in the pines and burned with hungry enthusiasm.

The heat lay on his cheeks, it crept beneath the blanket. The fawn lunged again, gasping for air. He put his weight across its back.

He heard a tree explode. Like a rifle shot it sounded above the roar of the fire, above the roar of the truck. Bits of burning wood came cascading into the truck. He wet a rag, and covering his hands he threw the burning brands to the roadbed and beat out the little fires they had started.

It had become a terrifying nightmare, and he was sobbing softly, though he never knew it. Then the truck stopped. Ethereal came back. He could see her only dimly through the smoke.

"There's a log in the road," she said. "We have to get it out of the way."

Without a word, Hurry Up crawled out from beneath the blanket and jumped down. Ethereal reached over for both the shovels. He grabbed the end of his mother's skirt and followed along when she walked through the smoke down the road.

The log was round about as a man's middle. "Here," Ethereal said, "we've got to wedge it out of the way. Put your shovel under this end."

She put her shovel beneath the log to show him. He got his shovel beneath the log as she had done. "Now. Now lift and roll it."

They lifted. The log slid, and then rolled a little. "Once more and maybe we can get around. They braced their shovels. "Now," she said. He strained. The log lifted a little, slid off the slant of their shovels and rolled about a foot. "Once more," Ethereal said. Both lifted and levered. The log rolled out of the way. They coughed, gasped for air.

"Quick," she said. Shovels went in first. Hurry Up clambered after them.

The truck seemed to be moving faster now, but the heat of the fire was becoming worse. Tiny tornadoes of flame picked up black ash and whirled it away into the sky of white smoke. Hurry Up poured what was left of the water over the fawn's head. Then he pulled the blanket all the way over himself and the animal.

Beneath the blanket he put his arms around the fawn and held it tightly. Now there was little oxygen anywhere because the fire was consuming it. Gradually then, the boy and the fawn lapsed into a semi-conscious state. For them the roar of the fire diminished, and only the pounding of his own heart was loud in Hurry Up's ears.

Later he could never remember outrunning the flames.

His first recollection of that desperate flight through the fire was lifting the blanket and seeing a white sign: "Otter City Memorial Hospital—emergency entrance."

He sat up then in time to see his mother help Mrs. Shoot First in through a door. A man in a white coat was with them, and he was saying: "Plenty of time. She's got plenty of time to have her baby in the hospital."

It was Mrs. Bear Paw who helped him down. Then his mother came back out. Her usually white face was brick red. He could see where the tears had streaked even her chin. She came right over and, taking the boy in her arms, said: "Oh, Hurry Up, we made it. We made it."

Mrs. Bear Paw was talking. "You sure did," she said, "you sure did, Mrs. Step-an'-a-half." Hurry Up didn't miss it. Mrs. Bear Paw had called his mother Mrs. Step-an'-a-half instead of Mrs. Hanson, and Ethereal was smiling when she said:

"Oh, thank you, Mrs. Bear Paw. Thank you."

EPILOGUE

Two days later it rained, and the people of Bloody Burn Bay went back. Some had been burned out, but they pitched tents. Some houses had miraculously been spared. Hurry Up's was one of these.

Immediately a meeting was called. Everyone came: Fish Fins Larrens, Ham Hocks Garrity, Four Toes Gregory, all of them and all their wives and all their children. Officials from the Department of Natural Resources at Madison came too.

For two hours they laid plans. New homes would go up before winter. In spring, new trees would be planted where the forest had been destroyed.

When the meeting was over, Step-an'-a-half and his son, Hurry Up, sat on the pier and looked out at a green island which had been spared. On the shore a leggy fawn stood watching.

"It'll all be like that again some day," Step-an'-a-half said, indicating with a sweep of his arm.

Hurry Up wondered how it could be.

"And you'll be surprised what a wonderful thing a new forest can be," the father continued. "All you've known is mature timberlands. When little trees grow, thousands more birds and animals come to live among them. For many years there is such a surplus of greenery close to the ground that the forest becomes a wildlife paradise."

Step-an'-a-half looked down and, seeing the doubt in his son's eyes, went on: "There'll be so many tens of thousands of snowshoe hares the owls won't have to hunt but five minutes to feed. Wolves will have a feast. Deer will have so much food they'll as likely as not drop twins their first breeding year and maybe triplets thereafter. And there'll be jackpine, because a roaring hot fire is the only thing which can crack the cones to scatter their seeds. And then," he said, looking off dreamily, "you may even see the rare Kirtland warbler whose life cycle seems to depend on the presence of immature jackpine."

The father started to talk again, but was interrupted when Ethereal called from the house. "Hurry Up," she called, "come here."

So he went up to the house.

"Those mice have built their nest in the cabinet again. Will you get them out for me?"

Hurry Up smiled, and he took the small mice in a kettle down to the pier and threw one into the water. At once Spade Face surfaced with a rush and went back down with the mouse.

Hurry Up laughed softly. He threw another and another until the muskie had eaten all.

The fawn came tentatively onto the pier. Its tiny hooves made a sharp, short sound everytime it put them down.

"No mice for the deer?" Step-an'-a-half asked.

"No. No mice for the deer," Hurry Up laughed. And then they were both laughing, and far across Bloody Burn Bay a loon answered.